"Susan Sizemore had created a fantastic vampire story that brings fresh life to the Nosferatu legends." —*BookBrowser*

"The Laws of the Blood series is deservedly becoming a cult favorite." —*Midwest Book Review*

"The author gives us a cast of memorable characters that are realistic, entertaining, and interesting." —*SF Site*

LAWS OF THE BLOOD:
Companions

"A juicy and tasty novel that whets the appetite for more works in this dynamite series." —*Midwest Book Review*

"A rousing adventure." —*Booklist*

LAWS OF THE BLOOD:
Deceptions

"An exciting vampire tale. Every book in the series is better than the last as the author continues to develop the culture of the vampire society." —*Midwest Book Review*

"The author knows how to write 'realistic' vampires. Her characters are three-dimensional and intriguing. Recommended." —*All About Romance*

"Readers will want to read this book more than once, but each time in one sitting!" —*BookBrowser*

"Susan Sizemore handles the traditions of vampire lore well, restructuring them in a way that makes a fertile ground for exploring (her) vampire civilization." —*SF Site*

LAWS
of the
BLOOD

HEROES

SUSAN SIZEMORE

2003
50TH
ANNIVERSARY

ACE BOOKS, NEW YORK

This is a work of fiction. Names, characters, places, and incidents either are the product of the author's imagination or are used fictitiously, and any resemblance to actual persons, living or dead, business establishments, events, or locales is entirely coincidental.

LAWS OF THE BLOOD: HEROES

An Ace Book / published by arrangement with the author

PRINTING HISTORY
Ace mass-market edition / October 2003

Copyright © 2003 by Susan Sizemore.
Cover art by Miro Sinovcic.

For information address: The Berkley Publishing Group, a division of Penguin Group (USA) Inc., 375 Hudson Street, New York, New York 10014.

ISBN: 0-441-01108-X

ACE®
Ace Books are published by The Berkley Publishing Group, a division of Penguin Group (USA) Inc., 375 Hudson Street, New York, New York 10014. ACE and the "A" design are trademarks belonging to Penguin Group (USA) Inc.

PRINTED IN THE UNITED STATES OF AMERICA

10 9 8 7 6 5 4 3 2 1

*For Juanita Nesbitt, vampire aficionado,
costumer, and all-around cool lady.*

Law: Beware of the Light.

Prologue

"ALL LAWS ARE lies!" Martina stood up and proclaimed.

Ben sighed. The outburst nearly annoyed him enough to ask the woman what the hell she was talking about, but that would give her an opening to tell him. He hadn't been following the conversation. Until a moment ago he'd been contentedly sipping a scotch and looking at the view from the meeting room in the hotel's penthouse owner's suite. Maybe the others at the table would just ignore her and go back to business.

Unfortunately, Dresser asked, "Why are you interrupting this meeting? What is it you want, girl?"

"A world without Enforcers," Martina promptly answered. "All Laws are lies," she repeated, and stuck her fist in the air.

She reminded Ben of Jane Fonda back in the Vietnam War era, but he managed to keep from telling the crazed vampire chick that as well. Martina and her whole nest were nuts. Fanatics. Death to the Pig Enforcers was their creed. Ben knew why Ibis had brought them in to manage the new hotel. Ben resented it, but he understood. The Silk Road had been open a little over a month and was running smoother than most new places usually did.

With the exception of his own nest, and that wasn't much of an exception, you couldn't get normal vampires to live and work in Las Vegas. Martina's crowd were at least focused on their cause. It helped them avoid the other dangers the city offered. His own people ran the casino and security for the whole Silk Road operation. They didn't have to deal with Martina's crowd that much. Ben only had to put up with her personally in these meetings, but that was more than enough. She really set his fangs on edge.

At the other end of the table, Ibis quietly cleared his throat. Ibis was always soft-spoken, but Ben listened when he talked. Along with everyone else, Ben turned his attention toward the owner of the Silk Road. Ibis was a small man, though he claimed he'd been average in his time, not that he ever said what his mortal time was. There was an ancientness about him, but he wore it as well as he did the dark, well-tailored suit. He kept his head shaved, and tended to wear eyeliner, but those were his only affectations. Most people might have pegged Ibis as gay back in his mortal life, but Ben knew for a fact that Ibis kept at least two female companions, and most of his slaves were girls as well.

Besides, once you became a vampire, gender distinctions didn't matter, even if mortal prejudices took a little longer to fade. Ben's were still fading, even though he found himself paying more and more attention to Morgan Reese since the stage magician brought his act to the hotel. Reese wasn't a pretty boy, or in any way feminine, but he had a glow of genuine psychic talent to him that made Ben's mating fangs ache. He wasn't yet sure if he was going to make a move on the magician or not.

All Laws are lies.

Ben jumped. He shook his head and glared at the old vampire.

Ibis nodded after he put that thought into all their minds. He steepled his fingers, caught Martina's gaze with his own, and said in his soft, subtle way, "I have heard that saying for centuries. It is true in most cases, of course, for mortals as much as for strigoi. Laws are necessary for the survival of a society, my dear. They have nothing to do with justice. You youngsters tend to hunger for such luxuries as justice and free will, when survival is the best one can hope for. And power, of course, but power has more to do with hard work and planning than it does with a passive concept like hope. We vampires are hungry all the time. Hunger for justice is good. Hunger for change is dangerous."

"I embrace the danger," Martina answered. "I don't hope. I plan."

And you shoot off your big mouth whenever you get a chance, Ben thought, carefully guarding his opinions from the others.

Ibis nodded. "I commend you for your dedication, Martini."

Martina hated the nickname, and studiously ignored the smiles and chuckles evoked by Ibis's use of it.

"But you don't embrace the fight for freedom," Martina said. Accused, rather.

"I don't attempt to hinder it," Ibis reminded her. "Your every word is against the Laws of the Blood, but do I try to silence you? I do believe in freedom of speech."

Martina sneered. It would have been impressive if there'd been a group of mortals sitting around the conference table. "You see the cause as my hobby."

Ibis shrugged. "Whatever gets you through the night. Now that you've interrupted real business," he went on, unlacing his fingers and putting his palms flat on the shiny black surface of the table, "tell us what it is you want, so we can get back to business."

Martina's sneer stayed in place. "Business. See what the Laws have brought us to?"

Prosperity. Civilization.

The words drifted through all their minds. Ben didn't catch the identity of which vampire had sent the thought, nor did he try very hard. Politics on any but the most local level of strigoi society didn't interest him.

"I want more," Martina stated.

Ben felt the annoyance and confusion that emanated from everyone but Ibis. Ibis was not in the least surprised, and answered, "You want more than our contract states. Let me guess, you ask the freedom of the streets of this city for your nest."

"We came seeking knowledge," Martina replied.

"It will take you years to discover all the treasures in my library."

"Knowledge can be found in other places than your ancient archive."

"Of course. You've decided that vampire history isn't really all that interesting."

Martina didn't notice Ibis's sarcasm. "Knowledge is of no use unless it informs action."

"If you say so." Ibis sounded particularly bored. He looked bored, but Ben saw the irritation in the old vampire's dark, dark eyes.

Ben took a sip of his drink. He wanted to get this over with, but he kept quiet. Restlessness and irritation sang through the room.

It was Dresser who finally demanded, "What are you getting at, Martina?"

"The freedom of the city."

"Why are you asking us?"

She sneered again, and gestured dramatically. "I ask Ibis."

Ben put his drink down hard on the shiny glass table. For the first time he spoke to the irritating female nest leader. "Ibis?"

It was the same soft, dangerous tone that sent chills through his enemies and subordinates back in his mortal life. Martina wasn't mortal, and she wasn't smart enough to recognize danger. What she probably saw when she looked at him was a young nest leader without power and prestige in strigoi society. She didn't know who she was dealing with, and she chose to ignore him, though Vegas was now and always had been his town.

Ben looked to Ibis, who gave him the faintest of conciliatory nods, but the owner of the Silk Road concentrated his attention on his troublesome hotel manager. "The traditional way of moving a nest into a new territory is to ask permission of the Enforcer of the City."

Of course, Martina laughed at this. "I do not deal with Enforcers. Not as a subordinate. You know that, Ibis. I do ask your approval."

Her gaze should have swept around to every other vampire in the room, but of course, she didn't bother. If she noticed the angry tension building at the table, she ignored it. Martina was not only a revolutionary, she was downright rude, or maybe just totally oblivious. She was up to something, of course, something to do with her schemes to change the world. The world was just fine as far as Ben was concerned, though it would be much better if Martina and her kind got out of town.

"What about Duke?" Dresser asked. "He's given permission for Martina's nest and ours to occupy the hotel. This is *our* territory." Dresser was one of about a dozen vampires that called Ibis nest leader. Martina had ten vampires in her nest. Even adding companions and slaves to this group, the vampire population took up only a small percent of the rooms and extensive grounds of Las Vegas's latest destination resort.

"You're not supposed to leave the area," Ben spoke up. "That's the deal."

"I did not make that deal," Martina answered. "I do

not deal with monsters who *eat* my kind. I am subject to
no Enforcer. To no Law set down by a puppet shadow
government."

"We've heard this before," Dresser complained.
"Maybe you don't obey the Laws, but Ibis does. You
agreed to work for Ibis in exchange for access to ancient
knowledge. Do you want to get him in trouble with the
Enforcer of the City?"

Martina laughed. "The Enforcer of this city is no
threat to anyone."

She was right about that, and Ben was thankful for it.
Duke, or the Duke of Norfolk, as he claimed to have
been back in his mortal life, was not what you'd call
conscientious. Above all else, the Enforcer of the City
wanted a quiet life.

"Just slip Duke a few thousand," Ben suggested.
"He'll be happy to leave you alone. I can arrange it for
you." *And take my usual twenty percent of the deal,* Ben
added to himself.

"I do not bribe corrupt monsters. I ask no one's permission to do as I choose. But yours," she added, concentrating on Ibis again. "Out of respect for your age
and learning, I ask the freedom of the entire territory."

Ibis rested his hands on the table. "I see."

"She's going to cause trouble," Dresser complained.

Ibis sighed. "I know." He kept his inscrutable gaze on
Martina.

This is my *town,* Ben thought. *She should ask me.*

"Do what you will," Ibis told Martina. When she
grinned with satisfaction, fangs gleaming brightly, he

added, "The consequences will be on your head, child, not mine."

There's going to be trouble all right, Ben thought. He sent a glare toward the happy Martina, who was about to spread her crazy revolution out onto *his* streets. He wondered just what he could do to help that trouble along.

.

Chapter 1

"LIGHT'S BEEN AROUND for a long time, of course."

"Well—yeah. You have heard of the Big Bang, haven't you?"

"I meant artificial light. Even when I was a youngster, there were certain—shall we say, weak-minded—individuals who'd have a little too much to drink and sit around staring into firelight for hours."

"Seems like a harmless hobby."

"Let me finish. It was hardly unknown for fire addicts to walk into a raging bonfire. The results were a bit—"

"Crispy?"

"Geoffrey, I'm not often in the mood to be instructive. Why don't you take me seriously when I am?"

"Sorry, Val." The truth was this was his first time in Vegas and what he really *wanted* to do was look at the lights.

"Oh."

Geoff Sterling was suddenly glad he wasn't the one driving the Cadillac convertible. He thought about closing his eyes, but the lights were so pretty . . . "Maybe you better continue being instructive."

"Uh-huh. Wise child." It was her turn to keep him out of trouble as he'd been doing with her for the last couple of years. "Being immortal doesn't make you invulnerable. There are certain—mental problems—that crop up from time to time in even the powerful, wise, and ancient ones. For example, I never thought I'd end up agoraphobic." The fact that they were in Las Vegas at all, and in a convertible with the top down, *and* that she was driving showed that the fear of open spaces was a treatable one. The fact that she was so scared she was having trouble keeping her hunting claws and fangs from growing showed that the phobia wasn't going away. It was just something, like all things that went with being a vampire, that had to be controlled. "Pain in the ass, really."

"What?"

"Nothing."

"I have noticed the death grip you have on the steering wheel." His head craned from side to side. Glitter everywhere! "Go on."

"Then there's light addiction," Valentine went on. "It's an ancient problem, but I have heard those who suffer from it called neon junkies. I'm afraid Las Vegas seems to attract a certain element." She paused, and finally stated, "It's a town full of losers."

Geoff felt her distaste, and he laughed, which pretty

much brought him out of his fascination with all the brightness and color filling the desert night. "Valentine, you are such a snob."

She tossed her head, stirring the thick fall of black curls around her shoulders. "Young man, I've worked in Hollywood for over seventy years. I wouldn't have stayed in the business if I was a snob about sleazeballs and losers."

"Hollywood sleazeballs and losers are mortal. You expect better from your own kind. Madam, you are a vampire elitist."

"I'll admit that I do prefer associating with a better class of monster, but I hardly think I'm snobbish."

"Uh-huh."

She ignored these sarcastic syllables. "All I'm saying is that light is a dangerous thing. While we're here, you need to be careful."

He lifted an eyebrow. "Just me?"

"Light's not my downfall. Probably not yours, either, but be warned, be aware. This place is dangerous."

"It's Las Vegas," he answered. "It's artificial."

"So are bullets," she reminded him. "So's a dagger, come to think of it. We tool-using types are very good at creating nonnatural recipes for disaster. Vampires have good reason to both bless and curse that Thomas Edison fellow."

Geoff turned his face into the hot wind that blew up the street out of the desert. "I like this town," he said. "It's a hungry place. Garish. Dark to the heart. I like that energy."

"It doesn't have a basketball team," Valentine complained. "How can you like a town without an NBA franchise?"

Geoff glanced at the fanciful architecture of the huge resorts on either side of Las Vegas Boulevard. He looked at the anonymous hordes of people on the sidewalks and the bridges crossing above the tangled traffic. He absorbed emotions and the essence of excited life. Adrenaline-soaked blood scented the night. You could get a buzz just from breathing around here. "It has other amenities."

"Doesn't feel that different than L.A. to me."

"You are old and jaded."

"No shit. Actually," she added, slowing the car, "something about this place is making my skin crawl."

Valentine ignored the honking behind them and the cars swerving to pass them. She slowed the Cadillac practically to a stop, her gaze swinging from left to right. "Oh," she said finally, concentrating on the nearest hotel. A many-domed palace set in exotic gardens rose above the street. It looked like ancient Samarkand had been set down on the Strip.

Valentine made a face. "So that's the Silk Road."

"Which is where we're staying, right?" Geoff began to suspect that leaving it up to Valentine to make their travel arrangements hadn't been such a good idea.

"Of course we're not staying there. Who wants to stay at a hotel run by vampires?" She stomped on the gas pedal.

"Uh, Val . . . ?" Geoff jerked a thumb as the building

receded in the distance. When she stopped at the next red light, he said, "We both invested in building the Silk Road."

"Yeah. So? I invested in White Star Lines once upon a time, but I didn't take the *Titanic,* did I?"

He looked back at the huge hotel complex. "You don't think it was a good investment?"

"I think it's a fine investment. And I'm sure it's a lovely hotel, if you want to pay five hundred a night for a room and you have absolutely no psychic ability whatsoever. I *know* what lives in that place, and personally, I've always hated being around vampires."

She sounded like she was talking about an infestation of cockroaches. "You said you weren't a snob."

"I lied. Of course, I don't like being around anybody—but you—for very long."

"Sometimes you give the term *reclusive* a bad name."

"I'm not reclusive. I'm a snob. You said so. At least about strigoi. Besides, our business is to work the room to get financing and distribution for our next project at the convention center at the other end of town. Why traipse back and forth from one end of Las Vegas to the other if we don't have to?"

"To see the lights and—shit." Geoff closed his eyes, then put his hands over them when he could still *feel* the light pulsing seductively just out of reach. "Shit," he muttered again.

"There's a Law," Valentine said. Her voice sounded very far away. "One of the few Laws that still make sense."

He was of the Nighthawk line. Nighthawks were supposed to be Enforcers, to know the Laws of the Blood. He'd opted not to be involved in the ancient system that constrained the lives of Nighthawks as much as it did normal strigoi. It wasn't as if he'd known he was going to turn into a Nighthawk. He'd only signed on to be a vampire, which was weird enough. The second change had come as a complete surprise.

He'd used his new powers only once, to avenge the death of someone he cared for, and that one time had been enough. He was a fledgling moviemaker, not a cop.

The car moved forward again and the hot wind continued to blow across his face while he waited for Val to explain. Instead, she let the silence drag on. Sometimes he worried about her attention span, or lack thereof, but sometimes, like tonight, she liked to play enigmatic font of ancient wisdom.

"What Law is that?" Valentine made him ask.

"Beware of the Light," she told him.

Geoff thought about it. "Maybe I should invest in some sunglasses."

"Maybe we should get you indoors and—oh, shit!"

The car swerved violently to the right. Brakes squealed. Horns blared. Geoff's eyes popped open as he was thrown sideways. Valentine was swearing, in a language that sounded kind of like English, but not much. Geoff saw her shaking her fist, and realized she was pissed as hell at somebody. He looked around, and saw a vampire dressed like a derelict standing in front of the car, staring into the headlights like a deer frozen on the highway. Only a deer's eyes didn't glow red with inner fire, and a deer's lips didn't draw back to show ugly yellow fangs. That was a couple of the ways you could tell a vampire from Bambi.

"Damn it, Eddie!" Valentine shouted in recognizable English this time. "Are you trying to get killed?"

"Eddie?"

A woman appeared out of the night before Valentine could answer, weaving between traffic with supernatural speed. The woman took Eddie by the arm in an unbreakable grip and led him away. Valentine let it happen, even though Eddie looked back at her with pleading eyes.

"Who was that?"

Valentine answered Geoff's question with a shake of her head, though her heart that had beat for several thousand years ached at the wrecked being that had lurched across her view. Was indeed. Eddie was so past tense. She wondered at seeing him, looming up like an accusing ghost out of one of Shakespeare's history plays. Wondered who the vampire female was. Wondered at what was going on. Valentine worried about him, but Eddie was long past any help.

"Neon junkie," she answered her young protégé. And drove on.

"You just want to gamble, right? After the wedding?"

"No."

"Jebel, you don't always have to be honest with me."

"Sweetheart, I am never completely honest with you."

"Good." Char McCairn considered this conversation, and decided she and Jebel Haven were being even odder than usual. She sat back against the leather passenger seat of the Jeep Cherokee and watched the long, flat desert highway roll by on the way from Arizona to Nevada as she said, "You aren't planning on robbing any casinos, are you?"

"Nope."

"Killing vampires?"

"Like shooting fish in a barrel in that town."

Jebel did like a challenge. She had her own plans for after they stood up for Santini and Della in the Las Vegas wedding chapel where they'd been told to meet the happy couple. "I just don't want you to get bored," she told her lover.

"Stuff happens when I get bored," he agreed.

"Fatalities happen."

Haven chuckled. "That's stuff."

"I'm glad Baker decided to drive his own car," she added as she noticed a pair of headlights when she glanced in the side mirror. She liked Baker well enough, but the big ex-cop had this tendency to try to kill her every now and then. No matter how often it was explained and demonstrated to him that not all vampires were bloodsucking fiends, he couldn't quite wrap his sense of self-preservation around it. He did try, but sharing close quarters with him didn't make for the most relaxing traveling arrangements for anyone involved. Besides, she enjoyed having time alone with Haven.

"How was Chicago?" she asked.

"Busy."

She could have ripped any information she wanted out of his mind, of course, but the struggle would be fierce, and terrible for their relationship. Besides, it wasn't the sort of thing she did. "I hate it when you get monosyllabic."

He turned his head long enough to give her a grin. "I know."

She bared fangs at him, and he laughed. "I love you, Hunter," he said.

Char basked in the words. Haven wasn't exactly vocal about his emotions, and his emotions were very rarely tender. He was a hard man. So hard that he'd been known to refer to her, a proud, fierce daughter of the Nighthawk line, as Little Mary Sunshine.

"How are you planning to spend your time?" she asked him.

He reached over to cover her hand with his. She liked how he always felt so warm. "Why don't we get a suite somewhere? The Palms? Bellagio? Wherever suits your fancy. Make it a private holiday."

She liked the sound of that. She also noticed he hadn't mentioned the Silk Road. Surely he knew about the place. Char gave Haven a very skeptical look. "What are you really up to?"

He had a deep, rough voice, and his laughter was the same. "Damn it, woman, when did you get to be so suspicious?"

"Since I met you."

"I've created a monster."

"No. Jimmy Bluecorn did that."

He gave a low, jealous growl that made her smile. That Haven could be so possessive without sharing a companion bloodbond with her flattered her. And it strengthened her opinion that a master-slave relationship between mortals and strigoi was unnecessary as well as demeaning. She also noticed that Haven didn't try to tell her that she wasn't a monster. She loved him for that.

"Did I really love Jimmy?" she murmured. "Or did he make me?" She was immediately assailed by guilt at such a disloyal thought toward her vampire sire.

Haven closed his fingers tightly over Char's hand when he felt her beginning to pull away. "Doesn't matter," he told her. "He's over and done with."

"That's true. There's nothing more ephemeral in the world than a vampire's relationship with a companion. Nothing more forbidden than continuing to be lovers after the rebirth." Char made a disgusted face. "Can't imagine wanting to—everything is so different—after."

Haven knew Char wanted to believe that a proper vampire like herself would never harbor any heretical thoughts. When it came to this Bluecorn dude, Haven was happy to encourage her orthodoxy. That didn't mean he didn't have questions about vampire beliefs. Not so long ago his attitude toward all supernatural creatures was that the only good monster was a dead one. He still held that belief a good seventy-five percent of the time, but lately he'd developed quite an interest in strigoi history and culture. Part of it was because it was smart to know your enemy. Some of it was simple curiosity.

"Who made up the laws?" he asked. "The Council?"

Good questions. When he was a vampire, he'd have an obligation to know the Laws. And respect those who enforced them—nest leaders and Nighthawks. For a mortal to know that the Council existed was against the Laws. It wasn't something even regular vampires were encouraged to think about, and never to question. Haven already knew more than he should. But not from her.

"Can't talk about it," she told him. "You know that."

"Won't."

"Can't." He continued to hold her hand, though she felt his frustration through this connection. "You're a monster hunter, Jebel, not a historian. I'll help you find the bad things out there—the things that need killing— I'll bend the Laws, but I won't break them. It would be fatal for both of us if I did," she added.

The problem with Char was that she actually believed in the boogeyman when she *was* the boogeyman— woman. He liked her the way she was, prim and proper and civilized, but he was an agent of chaos. "The Laws of the Blood are not for me."

"Not until you become a vampire," she agreed.

He didn't know if she just didn't get it, or was being deliberately obtuse, but Haven didn't push it. No one's laws were for him. Never had been. He didn't recall how many states had warrants out for him and he didn't care. He was an *outlaw*. Did Char really believe he'd become law abiding once he was a vampire? If he became a vampire.

When. It was only a matter of time before one of them gave in to the urge to share blood. Haven figured he'd be the one to crack. He'd considered killing her, especially when the urge to beg for a taste of her blood nearly drove him out of his mind. She'd told him that it would be heaven, and he believed her. He wasn't meant for heaven. Wasn't sure he wanted immortality. He didn't think he could kill her.

But he needed to know *how*.

That was one of the things he hoped to learn on this trip to Las Vegas.

Chapter 2

"Who was that woman?"

Eddie might have told Martina, if she hadn't hit him while she was asking. In his day women didn't hit people. People hit women, and that was the way it ought to be. The world was not fair or right and he wanted it to go back to behaving sanely instead of him being considered one of the crazy ones.

Eddie wiped blood from his mouth and licked it off his fingers. No use in wasting it. He dared to shoot a glance of hatred at the younger vampire, but saw his animosity bounce off the armor of her righteous superiority. Martina wanted to change the world. She'd decided he was going to help her, but she hadn't bothered to ask. He was one of the masses she was determined to save, but he was beneath her.

"Who was she, wraith?"

Wraith was the fancy name the revolutionaries gave the street ones, the light lovers. *Neon junkie* wasn't politically correct. Changing the words didn't change the facts. She'd probably never read Orwell. Or anyone else. Who read in this age? Who remembered that literacy was a tool of power?

"An old girlfriend," he answered before Martina hit him again. "From out of town."

Martina sneered, as though the notion of him having had lovers, or even friends, was ludicrous. "Will she interfere with us?"

"Did she stop and help when you were kidnapping me?" Did Martina recognize that Valentine wasn't mortal? Did she realize what Valentine was?

Martina laughed, though it sounded like something she thought she ought to do more than any genuine amusement. "Then let's forget about your *friend* and concentrate on what's important."

Eddie looked around the living room of his studio apartment. There was nothing important here. The place was shabby, but it wasn't squalid. He had a slave who saw to his comfort. Three slaves, two of them showgirls. He'd always had a thing for long-legged women. The slave who lived with him had been a showgirl once; now she stayed at home, gave blood, and did the housekeeping. He hated that Martina had ordered his slave to leave, and the woman had obeyed another vampire without question. The same way he'd obeyed. Both he and his slave knew he wasn't strong enough to do anything else.

"What is important?" he asked. "What do you want from me?"

She took a seat in his leather recliner. Sat in it straight and regal like she was queen of the world. "A great many things are important. Things you do not need to know."

Things he didn't want to know, he was sure. Fanatics were boring as hell. But this one was dangerous. "Fine. It's getting late." Couldn't she feel the sun? Maybe only the old ones, the light-sensitive ones, were truly always aware of the coming of the sun. "Tell me what you want and—"

"And what, wraith?" Martina lifted her head haughtily. "Are you trying to order me out of your"—she swept a hand through the air—"nest?"

He had a home, he didn't want a nest. Why did someone who was trying to change the rules of society have to have such conventional attitudes about how vampires were supposed to live? He didn't point out the inconsistency to Martina. She'd brought him here to show him she could invade his private dwelling with impunity. A common vampire power game.

"You're the one who brought me back here," he told her. "I wasn't planning on coming home so early."

He'd been heading toward Fremont Street when Martina first appeared in front of him. He'd sensed danger from her; madness radiated like heat off her body. Her thoughts were shielded, but swirling with wild schemes. He couldn't read details, but he knew she intended to drag him into her folly. He'd done her a few favors in the past, eighty years ago, back in Vienna. He'd heard she and her gang were in town, and had considered leaving. But how could he leave the light? He told himself she didn't know he was in Vegas. Stupid of him.

He'd run when he'd seen her, but Martina caught up fast enough. Now he was stuck with the crazy woman because she *was* stronger and smarter—and knew things about him it was safer others didn't know.

Martina rose elegantly from her chair. She did imperious well. Not as well as, say, Catherine the Great, but Martina was certainly better looking. Eddie wondered if Martini would ever get the hang of usurping and keeping power the way old dumpy Catherine had.

She spat. On his clean floor. He'd never known a woman to spit before.

"Hey."

"You know where the Duke sleeps," her voice cut across his complaint.

Eddie stared at Martina. "What? Why would I—?"

"Because you make it your business to know such things."

He made it his business to know everything. It was his business. Or had been until the light . . . It didn't look like he was going to get to drink any light tonight if he didn't shed Martina soon.

"What do you want with Duke?"

Martina stepped forward and put her hands on Eddie's shoulders. Her claws dug into his skin. "I'm going to kill an Enforcer," she told him. "And you're going to help me."

* * *

"What do you think, Clare?" Ben asked, whispering in her ear.

They were standing together, hip to hip, with his arm around her shoulder and hers around his waist at the very back of the dark theater, near the door. Smoke billowed on the stage, music blared as the audience applauded the performer's latest trick. Much of Ben's awareness was on the woman with him and the man on the stage, but his interest in them was also tempered by acute consciousness of the action in the casino behind him. The music of the slots was louder to him than the theater's sound system. The energy generated by the gamblers was a constant thrum on his psychic nerve endings. Right now it was an even, steady hum of greed and excitement, background noise, nothing for him to worry about. He could take these few minutes out of his night for domestic activities.

The look Clare gave him was amused. She had a beautiful heart-shaped face and full, red lips. "Tell me what you want me to think."

She was a companion, and as such didn't technically have a say in anything her master wanted. According to the Laws of the Blood, that is. Ben figured the Laws had been drafted by bachelors and old maids, or maybe just plain spouse-abusing assholes. 'Cause anyone who had a real relationship with a companion knew that the way to a peaceful life was to have a little give-and-take in the mix. There could be a lot of sneaking around, backbiting, and scheming in a nest where the boss didn't demand and give respect to the underlings. Ben had always run his nest as a business. He was the nest leader. He had the final say, and it could be a fatal say for any mortal that really got out of line if it had to be. But he listened to opinions, especially from companions.

Clare had been his number one squeeze for five years now. He valued her for her brains as much as for her body and blood and the psychic talent that was the spice a vampire needed to feed sexual hunger. He didn't taste her as often as when they first got together. That was because he intended to keep her attached to him for as long as possible. She was a genius with computers and all the high-tech security systems that were necessary in the casino business these days. No reason to turn her into a sex-crazed mush-brained baby vampire and lose her expertise any sooner than he had to.

The bloom had worn off their psychic connection, but he respected her place in his household. "What do you think of Reese?" he asked her again.

"As a magician or as a mate? Your mate," she added quickly when Ben shot out a burst of jealousy—jealousy that encompassed his possessiveness of both Clare and the mortal he hadn't yet taken.

Ben shook his head. "I'm not confused about anything, am I?"

"Of course not," she soothed his ego. "My master is always sure and confident. He's not that attractive," Clare added, looking back at the stage.

Even with the assistance of makeup, costuming, and stage lighting, Morgan Reese was not all that good looking. He had a good body thanks to hours spent working out, but he was on the short side. Ben knew that the man's hair was light red and thinning under the black rug he wore on stage. His mouth was small and his eyes narrow. None of this detracted from the high-wattage charisma that blasted out from the stage when he performed. Reese held the audience with a look, a gesture, his own personal magic, and he was a damn fine stage magician besides. Even though his Welsh wizard stage persona didn't exactly fit with the Silk Road's Central Asian fantasy theme, the magician packed every seat in the theater of the casino floor every performance, and sent happy customers back out to gamble the rest of the night away.

It was the scent of real magic that first brought Ben into the theater the night Reese's act opened. Curiosity quickly turned to personal interest.

"Looks aren't everything."

Clare grew tense, but after a few seconds' hesitation, she whispered, "His personality's not all that attractive, either."

Ben didn't disagree. Morgan Reese was all about Morgan Reese. He was all ego and arrogance, and ambition. The man wanted to get to the top of his profession, and would happily crush anyone who got in his way. "Reminds me of me."

Clare was genuinely indignant. "You're a nice man."

"I was a bastard when I was a man." He was frequently surprised at how he'd mellowed since he'd given up his life as a human being. He was still hard and ruthless and violent, but those were okay traits in a vampire. "The one who made me is a good person," he told Clare. "Her name's Alice. We met one night at Ciro's." At her questioning look he added, "Used to be a nightclub in Los Angeles. On Sunset. Anybody who was anybody went to Ciro's." He smiled reminiscently. "Alice made a project out of reforming me."

Vampires didn't often discuss their own histories; everything was supposed to be a big mystery. Everything. Much worse than any Cosa Nostra code of silence bullshit. With the mob it was always really about money; with vampires it was always really about perceptions of power. He didn't think it was about real power but personal power, which was stupid, but fine with him. And he thought that much of the secret nature of the society came down to many vampires not wanting to remember being forced to crave the rapes, beatings, and humiliations they'd endured as companions. Alice had tamed him, but she'd given him respect.

Clare drew his attention back to the present. "You going to make a project out of reforming Morgan Reese?"

He shrugged. "Maybe. Probably. What do you think?"

She bit her bottom lip for a moment, then said, picking up on his thoughts, "I think that people's real natures don't change, whether they're mortal or immortal. Who their master is and how they're treated as a companion influences the type of vampire they become—but pretty is as pretty does, as I'm told my great-grandmother always used to say. Reese ain't pretty. But he's hot," she added with a grin. "Sizzles with power. I understand your wanting to drink that."

Power he didn't know he had, Ben thought. "The stage magician doesn't know he's a real magician, does he?"

Clare shook her head. "I don't think he has a clue that the real stuff exists."

Yet Reese had been drawn to perform at the Silk Road, a place run by people made immortal by the use of ritual magic. Not only were the real magicians in charge, the vampire who owned the place collected magical artifacts and spell books and put some of the stuff on display as part of the hotel's décor. Reese was surrounded by magic, and it was only a matter of time before he was drawn into the real magical world. Ben intended to be the one who introduced Morgan Reese to the underneath world, but in a way that would make Reese want to be a part of it.

Ben stroked his chin as he watched the stage magician take a bow. Applause swelled, drowning out Ben's words as he said, "Maybe old Ibis's books and junk'll come in handy." He chuckled. "It'll be like inviting Reese up to see my etchings."

"What?" Clare asked. "I didn't hear you."

"Old joke," Ben answered, brushing her curiosity aside. "You don't need to understand."

The stripper's breasts looked hard as rocks; great mounds of flesh-covered silicon that stayed firmly in place no matter how much she gyrated and jiggled and whirled around the pole in the center of the little stage.

Haven didn't care that the boobs weren't exactly realistic. They were boobs, and he had trouble taking his eyes off them. Char had nice boobs. Not very big, but nice. He loved Char's boobs, but Char wasn't there, and her breasts would have been modestly covered if she was. And she would have been asleep, as it was eleven in the morning and vampires were not day people. So Jebel Haven sipped his second beer of the day and took uncomplicated enjoyment in the sight of a naked female as part of the bachelor party entertainment.

There was a conversation going on between the two other men at the table in the small strip club. Haven was aware of the sometimes tense, sometimes excited tone of his friends' voices, but he didn't give any of his attention to what they were saying. It became apparent that Baker and Santini wanted him on it when Baker waved a huge hand in front of Haven's face to get his attention.

Haven sighed, and peeled his gaze away from the woman on the stage.

Santini grinned at Haven, his bearded face as maniacal as ever. Maybe more. Della was no saint, even if she did run a homeless shelter. Marriage wasn't going to change the crazy biker. He raised his beer to his lips, drained it, then asked, "You wanna?"

Haven knew exactly what Santini meant. "Baker and you want to go hunting."

Santini glanced at the stage, and yawned. "Sounds like a better bachelor party than this. Getting married in

Vegas is a great idea. Thanks for thinking of it, Jebel."

"This town's swarming with vamps," Baker said. "Makes my skin crawl."

"Harmless," Haven said. "Most of 'em," he amended at Baker's annoyed look. "We've got a truce with the sentient ones," Haven pointed out.

"What's *sentient* mean?" Santini asked.

"*You've* got a truce," Baker said.

The three of them had formed their initial alliance to hunt and destroy a species of mindless bloodsuckers that inhabited the Southwestern desert. After a few years of killing what turned out to be a minor league nuisance of the monster world, Haven met Charlotte McCairn, vampire. Not only was Char a true vampire, she turned out to be an Enforcer, an ubervampire whose job it was to kill average vampires that got out of line. Char also felt a strong ethical need to police the rest of the underneath as well. And Haven was her enforcer.

Through Char they'd found out about the whole underneath world. That not only did vampires exist, but so did sorcerers, demons, werewolves, all sorts of monsters. Vampires had peace treaties and neutrality agreements with some of these creatures, but sometimes these monsters needed killing. Vampires couldn't do it—can't upset the balance of power in the underneath world, don't you know? Haven was happy to take on the bad guys Char couldn't technically touch. It was a lot of fun.

But vampires . . . Vampires needed something more complicated than merely killing. At least some of them. He'd tried to explain that to Baker, but Baker wasn't involved with the vampire culture. Baker couldn't understand.

Haven looked around irritably at his friends. "Couldn't we just get drunk? Get laid. Gamble. There's a lot more to do in Vegas than kill vampires." He focused his attention on Santini, *really* focused it, the telepathic way Char'd taught him. "What would Della think about you doing anything dangerous right now? She doesn't want her groom to get killed before the wedding. You don't want to go hunting right now."

Santini's eyes only glazed over a little as he nodded slowly to Haven's mental suggestions. "Yeah," he agreed. "Don't want to upset Della."

"You thought it'd be fun a minute ago," Baker said. He gave them a disgusted sneer. "You two are so whipped."

Haven shrugged. "I'm learning to be subtle is all," he explained. "We can't destroy vampires no matter how many we kill. There's other ways. Better ways." He leaned over and put his hand on Baker's arm. "Trust me." *I haven't deserted the cause,* he thought at the other man. Haven sat back and said, "Besides, I can't leave now." He glanced across the dim, almost empty room toward the door. "I'm expecting someone."

It would have been a nicely dramatic touch if the person he was waiting for walked in at that moment, but since it didn't happen, Haven went back to sipping beer and dividing his attention between his friends, the club entrance, and the entertainment. Nearly an hour passed before the door opened, letting in desert heat along with a woman.

Haven recognized her sharp chin and large mouth from the photo posted on her webpage. He didn't understand anybody letting their picture be posted on the web, or even letting their picture be taken if they could help it. Her photo was on an innocuous personal website, one that was full of blog entries about her daily life. Haven knew very well that the blog stuff was complete fiction. This woman's life was much like his own, too weird and secret for public consumption. He knew her by the screenname *Moll,* a name she used in sessions in a highly secure chatroom used by companions. Unlike the original members of the group, Moll had been recruited rather than having found them on her own. Moll was relatively new to his small, covert circle of online friends. It went without saying that she didn't have his complete trust even though he was one of the instigators of the new outreach program. He assumed that she didn't have complete faith in him. It took a lot to earn trust in their dangerous conspiracy to change the dark side of the world.

Neither Baker nor Santini questioned him when he got up and walked away from the table. That was mostly because he'd been learning how to use the psychic abilities he'd been born with. He didn't want them asking questions, and because they were each slightly psychic themselves, he was able to curb their curiosity, at least long enough to walk away unnoticed.

This small use of ability was enough to focus Moll's attention on him. They nodded to each other, and he joined her by the door.

"DesertDog?"

He gave her another nod. "Haven," he introduced himself.

"Murphy," she answered. "Clare Murphy." She gave a distasteful look around the setting. "Let's go somewhere private."

Haven already had a hand on her upper arm. "Fine." He steered her out the door, into the blistering heat and bright daylight. She shrugged him off and led him to a white Ford Explorer parked half a block from the club. As Clare Murphy unlocked the SUV's door, Haven asked, "What's so important about the Silk Road that needs a personal look around?"

Chapter 3

BEWARE OF THE Light.

The words kept running through Char's head, the letters huge and glowing like a bright, multicolored neon sign. Very distracting. The annoying part was that Char knew she was dreaming when what she was trying to do was project her consciousness out of her immobilized body instead of getting a good day's rest. Places to go, things to see. Just because she was physically stuck in an air-conditioned hotel room didn't mean she couldn't be mentally up and about—except when glitches like having her subconscious block her mind's way out of her body got in the way.

Yes, yes, Beware of the Light, I get it, she thought as she tried to will the images from her mind. The point was she wasn't interested in light. Enlightenment, yes, light, no. The sparkle and flash and neon glow of this city were all very well, but there was nothing resembling reality about the place. Char wanted substance, facts, knowledge. She had eternity to find out everything about everything, and was anxious to dig further into the most important subject of all: vampires, strigoi, her people. There was so much that was secret, lost, hidden, forbidden. Much of this attitude had to do with the nature of ritual magic, of course. Knowledge was indeed power, for those few people magic worked on. She appreciated the necessity of protecting powerful rituals and spells from those who would misuse them. What she hated was the hiding of history. Much of this history was forgotten as well as secret, she was sure, and that annoyed her more than the paranoia and gnosticism of her kind.

And she was thinking too much, and wallowing in her frustration while a neon sign blinked in front of her closed eyes. Action was what was needed.

What would Jebel do?

Take a shotgun to the sign, of course. Even in his dreams. It would never occur to him that he might give himself a bad headache that way. Char chuckled silently, and considered more sensible and subtle options for getting around her own mental roadblocks.

She closed her eyes, which was an odd thing to try considering that her physical eyes were shut tight and impossible to open before sunset. Her interior vision had been fixed on the bright, blinking neon sign even while her thoughts rambled. The first thing she had to do was block out the light. *Beware of the Light, indeed,* the words snarled through her thoughts.

Light still flashed behind her inner eyes, ominous, like lightning from an approaching storm.

Darkness, Char thought. *Nothing but lovely, still, velvet black darkness.*

It took a long time to come. She would have balled her fists in frustration if she could. She would have ground her teeth and drummed her heels against the hotel mattress. But stillness was forced on her. Stillness in the daylight was the nature and curse of her kind. She had to accept it as she had no other choice.

Gradually, the lights faded though they didn't completely disappear. Char also managed to push away from roaming thoughts and focus her concentration. The problem, she realized, was that she was trying to project her consciousness, but she was not trying to reach into the mind and movements of a waking person. Striking out on one's own without a carrier to dreamride was tricky.

She could reach Jebel easily enough if she tried, but what good would that do her in keeping this project secret?

Besides, he was busy today. He was attending Santini's bachelor party. The hardbitten mortal menfolk of her little world were carousing in ways she didn't want to know about. And it wouldn't only be rude to jump into Jebel's head and ask him to take her to the Silk Road. It would be dangerous to drag him into this. Not just for him trying to sneak into the areas she wanted to explore, but for strigoi kind if her mortal lover took an interest in her discoveries.

Char might disapprove of secrecy *within* the vampire community, but keeping secrets from those who did not have blood ties to the underneath world was imperative. Her involvement with Jebel Haven was definitely skirting the edges of legality for the two of them to be together the way they were. But it worked for them—

And she was thinking too much again.

Float in the darkness. *If you're going to think, think about where you want to be. Visualize, and go.* That was how this astral projection thing was supposed to work.

Like everywhere else, the Silk Road had a website. It had advertising brochures. There'd been an article full of glossy photos in a recent travel magazine, and she'd caught glimpses of the casino and lobby on a Travel Channel show on Las Vegas.

So, she knew what the place looked like. She only had to put herself there. Once she managed that, she could attempt to have a look around in the parts of the building where the tourists didn't go.

If what she wanted was really there.

Rumor claimed the archives of thousands of years of strigoi history were stored in vaults within the hotel. These records were guarded by an ancient one, and protected by powerful spells. Char hadn't been able to trace how this rumor had been started, or by whom, but it had come to her attention during her usual clandestine searching for all data relating to vampires. Char felt that it could all be a load of rubbish—or a trap. Why it might be a trap, and who might have set it, she didn't know, but something just didn't feel right. Still, insatiable hunger for knowledge more than blood or even justice drove her, and here she was. She would have come to Las Vegas even if the opportunity hadn't easily presented itself with the invitation to Della's wedding. Maybe it would have been easier if her curious and really quite bright Haven wasn't along for the trip.

Of course, she never had any intention of walking into the hotel run by vampires and asking to see this so-called secret chamber. There was no reason to behave stupidly. Enforcer she might be, one of the badass Nighthawk line, but she'd rather use brains and psychic ability and keep physical distance while checking the place out. She'd always kept a low profile, and didn't intend to change her method of operations—

I have got to turn off the word spigot in my head if I'm going to get out of my body anytime before sunset.

Char did not feel herself taking the deep breath as her lungs barely worked at this time of day, but she was very aware of the mental inhalation, of the strengthening of her will.

She imagined a door into daylight. She hadn't experienced daylight for over a decade, but it was not so long ago that she couldn't remember what day was like. She remembered sunlight on her skin, though she had to magnify the memory to account for climate differences. She was from Seattle, where a summer day was a very different thing than the searing brilliance of Nevada in the daytime. Fortunately she lived in Tucson now, so she had some concept of the Southwestern desert. Besides, she watched CSI religiously, and had rented the most recent version of *Ocean's Eleven* for research purposes before venturing to Las Vegas.

So she conjured the door, put her hand on the warm door handle, and fought off the panicked voice that screamed up from her instincts to *Beware of the Light!*

Char opened the door, and thrust her soul out of her body.

And screamed in terror and pain as the sun's molten fire poured down out of heaven to cover her in agony.

It wasn't technically possible to pace nervously around a room while lying immobile as a brick, but Geoff Sterling wasn't interested in technicalities. He wanted up. He wanted out.

He wasn't alone on the bed. Valentine was lying beside him. While his skin was cold and lifeless, faint warmth emanated from hers. He could feel it all along his side, both a subtle shock and comfort. But not comforting enough to stop this sudden restless panic.

He couldn't open his eyes to see his surroundings, yet he was vividly aware of every corner, every shadow; of the flimsy door and the wide window that overlooked the city far below. Heavy curtains kept out the daylight, kept in the coolness.

It was a perfectly suitable, ordinary upscale Las Vegas hotel room.

Anyone could get in. Anyone could find them.

Feels like a coffin, he thought, and wanted to claw desperately at the coffin's lid. He felt as if he were locked in one of those Victorian mausoleums where they left bells attached to coffin lids so the dead could ring them in case they woke up and needed to get out.

Or at least ring for room service.

The voice interrupting his thoughts was coolly amused, and thoroughly annoyed him.

We're vulnerable here, Geoff thought back. *Can't you feel the danger in the air?*

Valentine's silence was telling. *There's always danger in the air,* the thought finally drifted into his mind. *If you want to go sniffing for it.*

I mean for us. Here.

The door's locked, and warded. Don't be silly. You act like Van Helsing's lingering in the hallway.

Who?

Very funny. Go to sleep. Go dreamriding. Leave me alone.

I'm worried about protecting you.

We've got distribution meetings tonight. Worry about protecting me then.

Valentine's lack of concern was thoroughly irritating. Or maybe she was right and his paranoia was groundless. She hadn't mentioned the irony that she was the one normally reluctant to leave the safety of her Los Angeles lair—

Lair? Her sarcastic laughter was sharp in his mind.

If you can think about Van Helsing, I can use the term lair.

Lairs do not come with underground parking and swimming pools.

In L.A. they do. Besides, you never use the pool.

You do.

But it's not my lair. I'm only a guest ghoul.

You pay rent.

They shared the apartment. They shared their creativity. They kept each other company. They—

Go to sleep, Valentine urged.

Geoff realized she'd distracted him enough, relaxed him enough, that he was able to try. Back when he'd only been a vampire, before the surprising transformation from ordinary night creature to Nighthawk, oblivion had been easy. He'd had no choice. With the rising of the sun he was out, dead to the world until the first moment after dusk. He'd barely learned the ability to project his dreaming self into the daylight world before the Nighthawk compulsion took him. Now real sleep was the hardest thing for him to find.

Especially when, more often than not, finding real sleep resulted in daymares that always ended with Moira Chasen's screams.

Sometimes, like now, the dreams started with screaming.

He followed the sound. He couldn't help himself. *One moment he was drifting into darkness, the next sunlight hit him like a blow and he looked down to realize he was floating twenty stories above a busy Las Vegas street. Planes landing and taking off from the nearby airport whizzed by not that far over his head. Desert wind buffeted him, hot as flame. Geoff was tempted to scream himself as he whirled around, taking all this in. And then he began to fall.*

But the woman kept screaming, and he couldn't let it go on. He couldn't stop it with Moira, but this didn't sound like Moira. He couldn't plunge into the snarl of traffic without trying to—

"Where are you?" Geoff shouted as he fell. Below, he caught a glimpse of the lake in front of the Bellagio. The fountains were beginning the first water show of the day. From up here it looked rather odd. He fought his attention away from this distraction, and shouted again. "Wher—"

"Here!" The screamer's voice was hoarse and hysterical. "Who? Help!"

He followed the voice, caught onto the sound and followed it. One moment he was a spirit plunging uncontrollably out of his body, the next he was riding a sound wave. Cool. Something like dream riding, he decided, but different.

"Didn't know I could do this."

The woman screamed again. Then he saw her—a faraway speck of fire, falling like Icarus out of the sun.

The moment he saw her he was with her. He grabbed her, held her, stopped the fall. Flames swirled around them, but he didn't feel the fire. She wasn't mortal, he realized, and her being was no more substantial than his.

"This is so weird."

Her scream settled into a long, piteous moan.

Geoff shook her. "What is the matter with you?"

"Burning. The light. Hurts. Burning."

"Then stop it. You're not really on fire."

The woman held a flaming hand up before his face. *"Am too."*

"You're imagining it." Geoff noted that they were now floating in the air. The city stretched out below them. It was a funny-looking place full of fantastically shaped buildings, surreal as hell even without vampires hanging in the air.

"Burning," the woman said again. *"In the light."*

"Vampires don't do that," he reminded her. *"We're astral projecting,"* he told her. *"Dreaming. Change the dream."*

Char had no idea who this stranger was, but the other vampire's words made sense. She *was* dreaming. He was holding her, and they were—She closed her eyes, not wanting to look down, or around, or into the sun. She could feel his hands on her even when all other sensory impressions disappeared. *"How'd you get in my dream?"*

"How'd you get in mine? I heard you scream. You're still on fire," he pointed out.

"Sorry." She concentrated on putting herself out. *"Better?"*

"Much."

As Char's sense of panic ebbed, she recalled that her original purpose had been to astral project into the Silk Road. Clearly, they were not inside a hotel. With some effort she made herself open her eyes. *"There's a pyramid down there."*

"It's the Luxor."

"Oh." Of course, they were in—above—Las Vegas. Or dreaming that they were. None of it felt like a dream, but must be because she was manipulating reality. At least she wasn't on fire anymore. And they weren't plunging toward a blood-splattered, bone-shattered landing on the sun-baked concrete below.

She looked at the vampire holding her. Dark-haired, dark-eyed, pale—well, that went without saying. There was something familiar about him, though she was sure they'd never met before. Vampires frequently didn't meet, that was one of their problems.

"And protections," he said.

Char bridled. "Stay out of my head."

The other vampire glanced around. "I don't think that's possible, considering . . ."

Char concentrated very hard on keeping her thoughts secret, learning how to do it even as she thought about it. This was all very odd and disconcerting, but an amazing learning experience at the same time.

"I didn't know we could do this," the other vampire said.

"Neither did I," Char agreed. "I bet there's a great many things we don't know we can do." She didn't mean to say this, certainly not to a stranger. A stranger, yes, but—

She took a sharp breath, recognizing what was familiar about him.

Nighthawk!

The word screamed into his head with such force that

it pushed Geoff away from the woman. He grabbed his ears while the world spun. It took him a moment to realize he was falling.

When he righted himself, she was gone. The sky was empty. And he was still falling, slowly, gently, out of the light, into the dark, back to his body. He didn't fight it. This was too weird to go on for long. Exhausting.

He'd get a good day's sleep. Then he'd go looking for her.

Chapter 4

In the parking lot, Haven paused by his red Jeep Cherokee to take off the leather jacket he'd worn in the overly air-conditioned bar. The sleeveless black T-shirt he wore beneath the jacket hugged his body and bared muscular arms, the left decorated down most of its length with heavily inked black geometrical tattoos. He tilted his head up to hide his smirk when he saw Moll's eyes widen in horror at the sight of his choice of body décor. Maybe Clare Murphy had been expecting a gentleman.

"You're not a companion," Clare said, suddenly very wary. She took a step back from the Jeep.

Haven squinted into the bright blue sky. "You people always act like that's a bad thing. You asked me here," he reminded her. "Talk to me or not." He shrugged, then shaded his eyes with his hand, his attention drawn to a bright spot hovering in the air. He pointed at the light. "You see that?"

She turned to look. "What?"

"Like a—smudge—of fire." Whatever it was he saw, he didn't think he was seeing it with his eyes. He shook his head, trying to clear it. A cold finger ran up Haven's backbone, and something molten clutched in his gut. Something like a moment of hot jealousy. The emotion lasted a second, then, like the fire, it was gone.

"UFO?" Murphy suggested.

There was already enough crazy stuff in their lives; they didn't need aliens too. "Come on," he said, and opened the passenger side door for the companion. Like a gentleman. Despite throwing him a suspicious look, she didn't hesitate to get in. He went around to the driver's side, tossed his jacket in the back, then climbed behind the wheel and asked, "Where to?"

"Just drive," she said. "And we'll talk."

He drove. Past clubs, smaller casinos, and car dealerships. Eventually he found his way onto Interstate 15. Dust and heat haze swirled up in the distance, obscuring the view of the nearest mountain range. The woman beside him kept her silence until he finally asked, "This safe for you? Your—" He hated to say "Master," even if that was the right term for a vampire-companion relationship. He settled for, "—boss, occupied?"

"He's asleep. Dreaming of love." She let out a low, dark chuckle. "He's stalking a future companion. Ben's attention is not on me right now."

It didn't sound like it bothered her too much. "You

still better make this quick and get back to what you're supposed to be doing. What *are* you supposed to be doing?"

"Running security at the Silk Road hotel and casino. Our whole nest is involved in this one job. Only this job."

This did sound like it bothered her. "Think you ought to diversify?"

"We were diversified. He had a good business with a great reputation and more clients than we could handle. Then Ben gets a call from this Ibis the Ancient—"

"Ibis the Ancient? He really called that?"

She laughed. "Yes. Supposedly he's from ancient Egypt. There's a rumor that he's the father of all vampires."

"Is he?"

"Doubtful. I've only been able to trace his movements back a couple hundred years—"

"What with? Geneology dot com?"

"You're DesertDog, all right."

Haven gave her a sideways glance. "Recognize me by my sarcasm?"

"Yes. Can the wisecracks for now, please. I've got a lot to say and not much time to say it."

He appreciated the risk she took. Even if her vampire boyfriend was obsessing about someone else, there was always the chance some awareness of Clare would leak into the vampire's awareness. "Talk fast," Haven told her. "Can I ask questions?"

"At suitable intervals." She took a deep breath, fixed

her gaze on the road rolling ahead of them, and went on. "My initial interest in this meet was to talk about Ibis, and what he keeps at the Silk Road. It's important data, so I'll go through it first, then get to newer, much more important information the companions' group needs to be aware of."

"Much more important? Maybe you should—"

"No. Useful stuff for the rebellion first. Then we'll talk about the crisis."

This seemed like a stupid way of doing it to Haven, especially when she used words like *crisis,* but he doubted he'd get the intel from her any other way. "Go ahead."

"Never mind who he is or where he came from, the one true thing I've been able to discover about Ibis is that he's a collector of vampire memorabilia. He collects stuff, other vampires entrust it to him, he's got tons of stuff. It's said he can see the future."

"Stuff. What kind of stuff?"

"Documents, artifacts, data. Lots of historical data— stuff about vampires that should never have been written down."

This definitely piqued Haven's interest. He had no scholarly interest in vampire history, but he'd learned that knowledge was a weapon and he was very good with weapons. "You've seen this data? Examined it?"

"Not exactly." She held up a hand to keep him from interrupting. "What I've done is set up secondary security on the vaults where he keeps the important stuff, and primary security on the artifacts on display in the hotel." She shook her head. "Ibis is playing a huge joke, not only on the public, but on the strigoi."

"What's the joke?"

"The Silk Road's built around the theme that the place is a recreation of a mysterious Central Asian pleasure city. There are display cases full of artifacts supposedly found by an archaeological expedition from the nineteenth century. There are jewel-encrusted books full of untranslatable ancient writings, jewels the size of ostrich eggs, erotic wall paintings, gold ceremonial dishes, ritual weapons with carved bone handles and silver blades. Incredible stuff. It's all presented with a wink, of course, as a tall tale of wizards and lovely sorceresses with beauty so ethereal it could not survive the sun. It's all about moonlight and starlight. Very exotic and sensual—a place of earthly delights and magical wonder—without any mention of blood sacrifice and slavery."

Her matter-of-fact tone had become increasingly bitter. She paused for a moment, and took a few steadying breaths before she went on.

"I can tell you that none of the stuff in those cases is fake. Those artifacts are old, and they're authentic. The truth is, the Silk Road hotel and casino is based on the city the vampires built in Central Asia."

"The city—"

"Really existed," she finished for him. "I've gotten a good look at the magical artifacts. Ritual implements," she explained. "Heavy with magic. I don't know what the writing on the gold vessels says, but it twists my guts into knots to look at it. Most of the tourists don't notice, but

I've got lots of videotape of people passing by the cases. I can tell how much psychic ability anyone has by the looks on their faces." She gave a bitter laugh, and added, "There's a stage magician working in the hotel who gets a hard-on every time he goes near the display. Sick bastard doesn't know it yet, but he's going to be Ben's new companion. But the display cases are just for show."

"The books—are they spell books?"

"Very likely."

"Can you get at them?"

"I can. But unless we can translate them, it isn't worth the risk. It's the data Ibis keeps hidden that we need to access. There are secret histories, diaries, every kind of information we need to put ourselves on an equal footing with even master strigoi. Vampires are made by magic, but they aren't the only magic users in the world."

"I've encountered a crazy sorcerer," Haven admitted. "And a family of witches."

"You've met me. And yourself. You and I have the potential of using the same magic that vampires use—or we wouldn't have been picked to become vampires. I want to be able to acquire that magic to even up the balance between vampires and companions. I want a spell that'll make me an equal to Ben instead of his property. I want to find a spell that'll reverse the hold his blood has on me."

Excitement raced through Haven. "Do those spells exist? Does Ibis have them?" He wanted to ask if a spell existed to cure vampirism. Char might not think she needed a cure, but—

"That's what we need to find out."

"Is this a trap? An elaborate setup?"

"Good questions. I've been cautiously trying to find out, studying Ibis and his nest as much as possible. Doing my best to make friends with them. They're an odd bunch. Ibis is an odd duck."

"What makes him odder than any other vampire?"

"He's nice."

Char was nice. "He an absentminded scholar type?"

"Yes. And . . . Gentle. Wise. Amused. Kindly."

Haven snorted. "He's a bloodsucker. Does he keep slaves? Companions?"

"Yes. A lot. He has a huge nest. I think there may even be a waiting list of vampires wanting to get into his nest. But we both know that no matter how tight a ship a nest leader runs, how revered the master, there's always at least a hint of disgruntlement, resentment, or jealousy somewhere among the household. That's human nature, and no amount of blood, hypnotism, coercion, or torture can completely blot out individuality. Ibis's people all adore him, from senior nest vampire to newest slave. The other nest leaders working at the Silk Road respect him. Even that bitch Martina defers to him, though I think even he has trouble keeping her in line. Ben can't stand her," Murphy added.

Haven caught the contempt, and the fear, in the woman's voice. "Martina? She part of the crisis you mentioned?"

"Yes. She's head of a nest Ibis brought in to run the hotel."

His instant suspicion was that Clare Murphy had lured him to Las Vegas to get him involved in local nest politics. He knew that the nest Clare was part of was the only known viable nest in the city—until this Ibis and Martina showed up with their crews. "The Silk Road brought in outsiders, and your boss doesn't like them in his territory. That's your crisis?"

"Hell, no," she answered. "Ben was all for the project. The outsiders don't give him the respect he deserves yet, but that's his business, and he'll take care of it. I shouldn't have brought up Martina yet."

"Yet? If she's a danger to us—"

"She's a danger to the Enforcers. So are we," Clare added. "But not the way Martina is. We're going to be Enforcers." She gave him a sideways look. "I assume your vampire's a Nighthawk."

"Damn right," Haven admitted, and was surprised at the pride he felt in the reflected glory of Char's position in the vampire world. As usual, much of the surprise was in realizing how much he cared for her. He'd grown at ease with being in love, and that made him uneasy.

"All of us in the conspiracy are companions to Enforcers or potential Enforcers," Clare said. "At least as far as I've been able to determine."

"Not all of us are companions," Haven told her.

"But you're involved with an Enforcer."

"You didn't know I wasn't a companion until we met. There's a lot you don't know about—"

"I know that at least one of the online group is a vampire. Now I know that there's an unbitten psychic as well. We're all after the same thing. And we're all, more or less, kin to each other."

He raised an eyebrow at her. "Kin?"

"I belong to Ben. Ben was bloodchild to Alice Fraser. I've traced Alice's origin to a Nighthawk named Selim."

"*The* Selim? Enforcer of Los Angeles?"

"Yes. You have to be bloodchild of a Nighthawk to become a Nighthawk, though not all members of the Nighthawk line actually become Nighthawks—Enforcers."

"I know that."

He also knew that Siri, the woman who had organized the companions' group, was the current companion of the same Selim. Selena, who had really united the group as an active force, was companion to Istvan, the most powerful of the Enforcers. Yevgeny, the vampire member of the group, had told Haven that he'd been companion to a reclusive strig who was ancient, powerful, and had never hunted humans. Her prey was always vampires, which meant she had to be Nighthawk even if she lived outside the rules and regulations of the underneath.

"You might be right about most of the group. Maybe Nighthawk companions are different than regular companions."

"Maybe the Nighthawks subconsciously choose companions with stronger wills or—I don't know. What I do know is that all the Nighthawks are descended from the same person. All," Clare told him. "Whether it's a natural mutation or was caused by a magical incantation, I don't know. But I want to know, and I think Ibis has the answer. We need to know everything Ibis knows. We can't change the future until we understand the past—where vampires came from. What can and can't be done."

She sounded like Char. A whole lot like Char. "Knowledge is power, right?"

"Right."

Mostly, he thought firepower was power, but knowing the enemy did help in deciding the best weapons to use against it.

"So we're agreed that extracting data from Ibis's archives needs to be a priority for the companions' group?"

"Uh—sure."

"Good. Then let's table the Ibis discussion and get on to the more pressing problem."

"Fine."

Maybe others in the group might find this Ibis project interesting, but was it really that important? He wasn't the best person to try to break into Ibis's vault, or wherever the old vampire kept his stash of ancient wisdom. Haven had learned a little bit about computer hacking, but he was still better with a shotgun than with anything that required subtlety. Besides, wouldn't all these ancient texts be written in magical scripts and foreign languages? Still—Yevgeny was good with languages, and Selena could probably handle magic shit. He wouldn't mind being the muscle.

This really was Char stuff, but he couldn't exactly go to an Enforcer of the Laws and ask for her expertise to acquire intel for a companion rebellion. He'd decided long ago that she might sympathize with their goals, but the way the vampire world stood now, Char would react like any other Enforcer faced with a threat to the Laws. She'd have no mercy.

Haven noticed a sign for an exit a quarter mile up the highway. He decided to take it and turn back toward the city. Clare waited silently with her hands clasped tightly together in her lap until he made the turn. He wondered if it was his driving or the information she had to share that caused her white-knuckled nervousness. "Okay," he said when the surreal skyline of Las Vegas was in view again. "Tell me about Martina."

"She's an arrogant, fanatical bitch," were the first words out of Clare's mouth. "I don't mind that she's arrogant and bitchy, those tend to be exploitable weaknesses. It's the fanatical part that's dangerous."

"Fanaticism's a weakness," Haven answered. "What's she fanatical about?"

"Enforcers. Hates 'em. She's out to destroy the Laws, and the entire structure of the vampire world."

Haven didn't see what the problem was. "And we're not?"

"Martina doesn't think Nighthawks are true vampires. She wants to kill them all. Not just the Enforcers, but the whole bloodline. We have to stop her from killing the vampires we love. And destroying our potential future at the top of the strigoi food chain."

Maybe the Enforcers posed a threat to the companion conspiracy, but who the hell would ride herd on vampires hunting humans if not the Enforcers?

Haven snarled at the thought of any vampire trying to harm Char. "Okay," he said, slowing the Jeep as he eased his foot back on the gas pedal. Maybe he wasn't in such a hurry to get the woman back to her car. "We've got a crisis. I'm listening."

Chapter 5

"I'M SUPPOSED TO be in rehearsal."

Ben watched Morgan Reese as the man ran a finger down his jaw and finished by rubbing his chin. The gesture held grace that was for once not conscious or calculated, which Ben found far more attractive than Reese's usual mannerisms. Even better, Reese's genuine confusion and sudden loss of self-confidence were delicious stimulants to Ben's psychic senses.

Reese didn't know why or how he'd gotten from the theater and up the wide sweeping staircase to the entrance of the hotel museum, but Ben did. Ben had leaned against the wall, folded his arms, closed his eyes, ignored the crowds of tourists, the guards that were his property, and the concealed cameras that were monitored by his property, and *wished* for the mortal man to meet him in this spot.

Ben had almost been surprised when Reese appeared at the bottom of the stairs, but he'd been more pleased and sure of his control with every slow step the magician took up the staircase. Ben caught the man's gaze and held it, reeling the mortal in with his will. When Reese reached him, Ben almost took his hand, but recalled in time that they were in public. Ben was used to being in the closet in one way, but this was a new wrinkle in his existence. He frowned, hating the notion of one more aspect of his life he needed to conceal.

Reese noticed Ben's annoyance, and took a step back. "What's wrong?"

Ben heard Reese's resentment at being intimidated, and that made him smile. Ben checked his watch. "You've got two hours. I'm going to give you a private tour." He gestured toward the museum doors.

They shone with blood red lacquer and gilt and were ornately carved with Asian dragons and tigers and the sinuous script of some forgotten language, all of this studded with jewels for emphasis. Ben was used to Las Vegas excess, but this décor was something else. Because the doors really were what the publicity claimed them to be: the entrance to an ancient pleasure palace. Ben had never thought he'd be impressed by the kind of stuff Ibis brought out of storage for the exhibit, but he had to admit it was all kind of cool.

He saw excitement light Reese's eyes, and knew that Ibis's collection was not only cool, but also seductive. You could lure most women by being powerful, Ben thought, get her hot and bothered by what you could give her. Men like Reese wanted power for themselves, and could be seduced by the promise of it. Ben could and would give Morgan Reese the gift and power of immortality, but Reese would belong to him body and soul first. Fair was fair, and you paid for the privilege of living forever. Those were the rules, but Ben was gentleman enough to show his dates a good time before taking them back to his place for a bite. He was a vampire, for God's sake, not a rapist.

Reese blinked and the blankness left his expression. "I've seen you around. You work in the pit."

Ben was both surprised and amused as he realized that while he was obsessively aware of everything about Morgan Reese, including where he was at every moment of the night and day, they hadn't met before now.

"I run the pit," Ben told Reese. "I run a lot of things." A cold look came into Reese's eyes, and he looked like he was about to sneer, but Ben stared down this hint of rebellion. "Let's not fight on our first date."

He turned toward the doors, and Reese accompanied him without question. Except for the dramatically lit cases, the lighting in the exhibit hall was subdued. The thick carpet made movement comfortable and silent; the acoustics absorbed noise. The silence lent to the air of mystery. It wasn't crowded inside the hall. This time of day there were more people at the hotel's buffet tables than strolling through the exhibit. Ben's stern thought to leave sent a few more tourists away.

"The world would be a better place for vampires if everybody responded to magic." Ben spoke quietly, certain that Reese was the only one who heard him. When he got the expected startled look, Ben chuckled.

He took the magician by the arm and led him to one of the cases. A cracked earthenware bowl and a few parchment scrolls that had definitely seen better days rested on a bed of golden sand behind the thick clear walls. Ben pressed the silver button on the shiny black base of the display. This brought up the narration, a rich, clear voice that spoke seemingly out of nowhere, almost like a thought that popped directly into the listener's head.

"If you think the ancient gold coins in the next case have more value than my ragged and cracked contents, then, my friend, you are gravely mistaken. Worse, you are beyond interest. Gold is an instrument of power, but only on the most mundane of levels. Real power is not for everyone. What I contain is not for everyone. Few have the ability to appreciate what I hold. Fewer still the inborn ability to use it. What do I hold? Magic. Real magic. Real power. Reality as it really is."

"Yeah, yeah, yeah," Ben said, and pulled Reese back a couple steps, out of the range of the speakers. "It's true, though," he told the stage magician. "What you do is tricks and crap. But you already know that—in your bones and blood."

Arrogant fury formed a dark halo around the magician. "Who do you—?"

"You're here because I want you here. You can't walk away from me even though you want to. Go ahead, try."

Reese had a strong will and great latent talent. Actually, the talent was very close to the surface, but the man knew how to use it only from a stage. He fought hard to get away from Ben, and Ben loved the fight. He kept calm, though, kept the glee, the turn-on, from showing. There was enough energy generated in the few seconds Reese fought him for very other vampire in the hotel to be aware of what was going on. They probably had headaches. Ben certainly did, but he stood there and smiled, and waited.

Sweat covered the magician's face, his muscles tensed, then slowly relaxed. Finally, Reese said, "What the hell are you?"

"A friend. Your teacher."

"Teacher?"

"What you could learn—" Ben shrugged, while Reese stared at him, annoyance warring with sly curiosity. "You feel the power in here, don't you?" Ben asked the other man. He knew for a fact that Reese was drawn to this place. Clare had shown him the surveillance tapes documenting Morgan Reese visiting the museum over and over again.

"Yes," Reese answered slowly. Ben let the man's gaze drift away from him, back to the objects in the case. "They call to me. I want to break the glass—"

"It's a lot stronger than glass."

"—and touch them. I have this—dream—that if I could figure out how to use these props . . ." He shook his head.

"I can teach you how to use them." This was a lie. Ben neither knew nor cared about the old-fashioned magical knowledge stored in the hotel. "You belong here," Ben told Reese, stepping closer. "With me."

"Oh, isn't that sweet?"

Ben whirled at the sound of Martina's voice. He hadn't heard or felt her approach, and this annoyed him as much as the interruption.

She looked at him with a disdainful sneer. "Am I interrupting a romantic moment?" The sneer turned into a nasty smile. "Good." She put her hands on her hips and looked Morgan Reese over. Ben's fists knotted, and his hunting fangs began to edge from their sheaths, but Martina's gaze flicked dismissively away from Reese before Ben had to defend his property. "Ugly bit of owl bait," she said. "Shouldn't you be working?" she asked Ben.

Ben very much wanted to slash his claws across the bitch's face, but he held his temper. As head of hotel security, he would set a bad example by getting into a physical fight. He'd find another way.

He didn't think she was even trying to provoke him, not on any personal level. Martina simply held any vampire that wasn't one of her followers in complete contempt. She was nuts, but oh, how he would love to see her take a fall.

"My nest know their jobs," Ben told Martina. "We've worked casino security since the days guards patrolled catwalks over the casino floors."

"Really? She sounded exceedingly bored with this reminder that she was in Ben's territory. "Are you sure this courtship of yours isn't interfering with your nest's efficiency?" she added.

"I'm sure." Ben laughed. "Are you sure it isn't inter-fering with *your* nest's efficiency? It occurs to me that maybe you're here because you wanted a look at my boy. He's got one or two of your people in heat, doesn't he? A little bit of lust slowing down the vampire revolution?"

Martina glanced back at Reese, who stood still as stone while the vampires talked about him. Reese was tense and angry, but Ben held a tight mental leash around the mortal.

"The revolution will not be slowed by anything," Martina announced. "Even our lust is regulated by the Enforcers," she went on, didactic as ever. "We must have permission from them to choose who we will pos-sess, who we own, who we will love."

"That's not exactly true and you know it."

Ben could have hit himself for responding. Get the woman started on Enforcers and there was no stopping her. Hell, there was no stopping her anyway. At least she kept her voice down, as did he, and no one but Reese was anywhere near them. He still should have shut up, but instead he found himself defending the system.

"The Enforcer of this city doesn't pull that permis-sion shit. Duke doesn't care who we take."

"Soon your Duke won't care about anything ever again."

There was a thread of triumph moving through her emotions. Some menace and promise that went beyond her usual threats. Ben didn't want to know. He didn't want to be involved. He did want the bitch out of his hair. Out of his town would be even better. For now, he'd settle for keeping her from spoiling his date.

She read the surface of his thoughts. "Don't worry," she said, and gestured toward the case. "I told Cassio I'd meet him here. He's delivering a translation of those scrolls."

Cassio was one of Ibis's nest flunkies. He called himself the Chief Librarian, and he liked to speak Latin. Ben knew him from the pit. Cassio liked to gamble, and he liked to cheat, and it was no problem letting him get away with it. Cassio never collected his winnings; he just liked beating the house. Ben and Cassio got along fine.

"A translation, huh? In English?" Ben glanced at Reese. The magician was wide-eyed, and he looked scared. No doubt he was taking in the conversation and coming to realize that their open mention of vampires might be more than crazy talk, and that it might not bode well for him—a witness to an argument between a pair of vampires.

"English," Martina confirmed.

"The Council forbids translations of spell books."

"I know that. Cassio knows it. Ibis knows it. But the truth cannot be hidden forever."

Ben put a hand on Reese's shoulder. The man radiated power like pent-up lightning. "You know, I agree with you on this one." Ben hadn't known how he was going to pay up on his promise of revealing real magic to the stage magician, but now it looked like it might be easy. He'd have a little talk with Cassio about getting his own copy later.

In the meantime, Ben made the best of it. He even managed a falsely sincere smile for Martina. "I'll leave you to your meeting."

She was smugly pleased that he'd said he agreed with her on something, and gave him a grand, gracious nod in response. Ben half expected her to give a little stiff-fingered queen of England wave.

"Come on," he said, guiding Reese away from the crazy vampire woman. "I'll walk you to the theater."

Chapter 6

"THIS DOESN'T FEEL right."

Geoff watched Valentine as she paced back in front of the window of their hotel room, her bare feet padding silently on the thick carpet. The lights of the city glowed below, bright and beckoning. "You are not unaware of the irony of our changing places, are you?"

She stopped and glowered at him. For a moment she looked confused, then she said, "You mean I'm as nervous now as you were before we went to sleep last day?"

"Yep." He leaned back on the bed, supporting his weight on his elbows. He gazed up at the ceiling, aware that she was staring at him on more than a physical level. "I'm fine now," he added.

"Uh-huh," Valentine answered slowly. "And full of plans and schemes that have nothing to do with our reason for being in town. I told you Las Vegas was seductive—"

"You warned me about the lights," he corrected.

"Same thing."

"Is not."

Valentine grinned. "This isn't getting us anywhere, but it's kind of fun."

He sat up, and glanced at his watch. "We're supposed to be at a party. You're not dressed yet."

"Going out doesn't feel right."

"That's not what you meant."

"But it's my story, and I'm sticking to it. I hate parties. I should never have let you talk me into this."

"You liked the idea until we got here."

"There's nothing going on at the party that we can't deal with in a few calls."

"We should put in an appearance. Not like that," he added.

She was wearing an old Lakers' T-shirt and thong underwear. Her black curls were tousled, and there was a glow about her full lips and dark eyes that made her look like she'd spent the day having wild sex when he knew very well she'd been lying beside him, as out for the daylight hours as he was. Of course, it was likely Valentine's interior life during the day had been as interesting as his had been.

"No, it wasn't," she answered his thought. "I always look this good. You don't always notice. You look lovely yourself this evening, Mr. Sterling."

At her sarcastic tone, Geoff looked at his reflection in

the mirror across from the bed. Even though he'd showered and shaved and put on a black shirt, pants, and jacket, he looked about as wasted as he felt. He ran a hand across his face. "There was a girl," he muttered.

"A classic opening line," Valentine, ever the storyteller, supplied.

He gave her a dirty look. "What were you doing while I was—"

"Up in the air? That was a nice trick, by the way. I only caught a bit of it, but the effect was mighty strange. Not quite a dream, certainly not a dreamride. Who was the girl?"

"I have no idea." He intended to find out. Needed to find out. Something about her called, blood to blood. "She was one of us," he added.

"Of course she was."

"One of yours," he clarified. "Nighthawk." He rubbed his face again, and a thought occurred to him. "Enforcer of the City? Is the Enforcer of Las Vegas a woman?"

"I don't keep track of such things. No Enforcer stays in Vegas for long. Last I heard, it was an old boy the Council almost literally dug up off an old English estate and put to work. That was twenty years ago. Don't know if the old duke is still around."

"Maybe they brought in someone new," Geoff said thoughtfully. "Someone fresh and smart, because of the Silk Road."

"Maybe. No business of ours," she reminded him. "We're here for a convention. Which reminds me . . ." She pulled off her T-shirt as she marched toward the bathroom. She had magnificent breasts and he enjoyed watching them as she moved past him. "We're supposed to be at a party," she added, before closing the door.

Geoff waited until he heard water running in the shower before he stood. The room felt too small. The idea of spending the night socializing and doing business with mortals was too small as well. He wandered to the window, where the lights below called to him. He could feel the heat and sizzle of neon in his blood, like a drug. He closed his eyes against the siren brightness, and decided he was going to have to get a pair of sunglasses.

Something more important than production and distribution deals was going on out in the city. Something fit for a vampire's energy. He hadn't felt the need to hunt singe his blood for a long time. But the craving was there under the stunted, grieving surface, wasn't it? He hadn't wanted the way only strigoi could want since Moira's death, or at least he hadn't let himself.

"I would have given her immortality." He ran a finger down the cool surface of glass, the claw extended without his thinking about it.

Moira had been so weak, so vulnerable. She'd never had a chance against the nest that hunted, raped, killed, and consumed her. Prey. Rightful prey. Damn the Laws, and all those who enforced them. At least the Enforcer of Los Angeles had seen the injustice, had allowed Geoff his revenge. So, he couldn't damn all the Enforcers. He couldn't be one of them, either.

The woman he'd held in his arms high over the city

was an Enforcer. Or at least she was a Nighthawk. He
wanted to see her again.

Like calling to like? he wondered.

If nothing else, he wanted—needed—to know what
they'd done and how.

If he thought about it hard enough, he could probably
trace her. There was a scent about her, mental and physical, that was strong, familiar, and intoxicating. She'd
sparkled. Hell, she'd *burned.* And she'd run—the scent
of fear was the easiest to follow. He could find her.

He nodded at his faint reflection in the window glass.
And he stared into the night and took a deep breath. He
scented a kaleidoscope of life and blood and energy of
all types and kinds. Out on the streets was the easiest
place to start.

Valentine was going to have to go to the party without him.

"Why am I not surprised?"

Valentine looked around the room one more time, not
that she really thought Geoff was standing in a corner
waiting for her with the shadows pulled around him like
Dracula's cloak. No, he was gone all right. It wasn't that
she minded, exactly, it was just that his running off into
the night without her was so predictable.

She didn't want to go to the party either. She was
committed to tonight's affair only for Geoff's sake. He
was trying to cure her nervousness about being around
people. Mostly she suffered from genuine agoraphobia,
but there were other reasons she'd tried to swear off par-

ties. When she went to parties, she met people. Meeting people led to trouble, especially for the people she met. Brought home. Bit.

Fortunately for the mortal population of the planet, she wasn't feeling particularly horny at the moment. Fortunately for the vampire population, she wasn't feeling particularly hungry.

What she felt was—restless. Dreadfully restless. Restlessly dreadful? A restless sense of dread?

Valentine nodded. Yes, that covered the mood. *Something* was going to happen. Something was always going to happen, of course. Maybe she spent most of her life safely ensconced in her apartment, but that didn't mean she wasn't aware from a distance of all the twitches and tribulations that rode the psychic links which tangled her up with all her children. Generally, she tried not to tap into it, except for the occasional story idea. Too bad there was so little new to tell. Life was a soap opera, vampire life even more so. Eternity was the stuff of drama—and Valentine had always preferred comedy.

"Or at least satire."

She pressed her lips together firmly, adding annoyed at talking to herself to her general annoyance. At least if Geoff were here, she could hold a conversation with someone else. Not that she actually needed another's physical presence to hold conversations. If she wanted to talk to Geoffrey Sterling, all she had to do was reach out her mind.

And if she did that, she was likely to become aware of

other vampire minds out there, not all of them the sort of persons she wanted any contact with.

Take Eddie, for example. Valentine had taken him a lot once upon a time. He'd never been a favorite of hers, but the pickings for companions were rather slim after the Black Death swept through the world.

She remembered even now how dark the world had been then. Even for those like herself who dwelled in the night, the darkness had been suffocating. Darkness of spirit, darkness of hope had been all around. Decay and silence everywhere. But it was a painful silence that came hard and heavy after the cries for mercy rose to heaven, then turned to curses, to rattles of death and wails of mourning.

The world of the Plague years existed in the sort of death-saturated atmosphere your modern Goth types would consider vamp heaven, but it hadn't been any fun at all. There weren't even that many vampires in the world at the time of the Black Death. So, even if it had been a vampire party waiting to happen, there wouldn't have been many guests to exploit the pain and anarchy of the suffering mortal world.

The grand experiment of a vampire city-state had died less than a century before. Most of the vampires in the world were destroyed when the Asian city fell. Valentine hadn't been there. She didn't know exactly what happened, but she hadn't mourned when what few refugees there were brought word of the city's demise. She hadn't thought founding the city was a good idea to begin with. Nothing good came from the insularity and growing decadence of the place as far as she was concerned. If the Mongols hadn't shown up to tear down the city walls, it would have blown up from the inside from slave rebellion or the experiments with dark magic.

There were rumors that slaves and companions had revolted, letting the Mongols into the city. Those rumors, and much other knowledge, had been ruthlessly quashed and hidden by the Council that was formed to regulate the survivors of the city.

Of course, no one asked the strigoi who'd never lived in the city to be on this new ruling Council. Most of the noncity vampires continued about their business, paying no attention to the refugees' pretensions.

When the refugees moved into Europe, Valentine took herself across the Channel to visit the White Lady, who'd been Nighthawk and Protector of the Isles since Roman times. The Lady didn't hold with any foreign vampires in her territory, but she made an exception for Valentine, who was, after all, the bloodmother of the vampire that had sired the Lady herself.

Valentine took up the life of a traveling minstrel, but at exactly the wrong time. As she roamed the country, she bore witness to the Plague running like wildfire through the towns and fiefdoms. Many, many of the Black Death's victims were those born with psychic gifts. Vampires could not be touched by the Plague, but those born with the ability to be reborn into the vampire life were particularly susceptible to it. Valentine felt those deaths and mourned them, each one the passing of a child she would never have. It brought her to one of those black times in every immortal life where she would have welcomed her own passing.

Then she met Edward. He was a feudal lord with a retinue reduced to a handful by the Plague. She'd felt the magic in him as she approached the castle where he'd hidden himself away. He was light after so much darkness. A feeble light, but enough to make a companion. Enough light to save her from her own growing darkness.

After several years of sharing bed and blood, she'd sent him out into the night a new-made vampire, to be nurtured in the nest of the White Lady, who released him into the night as soon as possible, Valentine heard. His transition into the underneath had not been one of Valentine's success stories. He'd been a born user, a petty schemer, lived his life as a noble without any noble intentions as a mortal. He hadn't gotten any better with time. That he'd ended up a neon junkie in Vegas didn't surprise Valentine at all.

She could feel him out there in the night, all grimy, greasy, and covered in fear sweat. She wondered what it was he had to be afraid of. She reminded herself it was none of her business. She also noticed that she was standing facing the closet, her back to the window and the outside world.

So, what were her choices for the evening? She could stay here with the curtains closed and be perfectly content. She could put on a slinky black dress and attend the party Geoff had already ducked out on. She could check up on Eddie . . . but the idiot was an over-six-hundred-year-old grown man responsible for his own life.

Of course, knowing Eddie, if he was in trouble, it was because he'd gotten someone else into even more trouble. She knew all about the Rasputin business, and some of the other scams he'd been involved in.

He's a neon junkie now, she told herself, not causing anyone trouble but himself. Then again, the atmosphere in this town was positively *fraught* with impending weirdness. She did not want to wonder what was up, but she did. And if anybody was going to be involved with nasty goings-on, it would be her old pal Eddie.

Valentine's conscience, and curiosity, nagged at her enough so that she took a seat on the edge of the bed, and closed her eyes. If any information flowed in out of the night, she'd absorb it. It wasn't as if she was obligated to *do* anything about it.

Chapter 7

"WE HAVE HIM."

There was more she wanted from him or she wouldn't be here. "I don't want to hear about this." He wanted to put his hands over his ears, but then he'd miss the music. He liked the way the music blended with the lights, and it was about to start. He wanted to look up and live in the lights. He didn't want to look at her. But she put her hands on his shoulders and shook him.

"There are too many cattle here," she said. "Come with me."

She took his arm and pulled him down the street, into the darkness of a parking garage. He could hear the music start in the distance. He whimpered, missing the lights. Needing them.

"I want your help."

He glared at the tall woman. The power in her was al-

most visible, almost glowing. She didn't have enough light to satisfy him, but he had no choice but to look at her now. "I've helped you."

"Not enough."

"It will never be enough for you."

"No," she agreed. "We must all serve—until we are all free."

"Yeah, yeah." Cynicism, and his own needs, were armor against her idealism. "I told you where he sleeps. That was enough."

"Having him isn't enough. We need a place to keep him."

"You didn't arrange that already?" Stupid woman. Stupid, plotting, plodding woman.

"One thing at a time. We had to capture him first, make sure he could be held." She put her hands on his shoulders, but at least she didn't start shaking him again. Her touch was mild, her voice even made an attempt to sound friendly. "Rumor says you have a place. The exact sort of place we need."

Damn. He thought he'd covered his tracks better than that. "It's an old rumor."

"Of an old place, an abandoned place where my slaves can work. We'll take him there. Show me the way."

It wasn't a request. Nothing was ever a request with this woman. He didn't even know if the building was still standing. He doubted she'd offer to pay him any rent. "I don't remember—"

"Yes, you do." Now she shook him. Then she laughed, low and ugly. "Be good, light sucker, and I'll let you

play with a flashlight if you do what I say. Soon we will
have physical proof. Then all we will need is the Scrolls
of Silk."

"My, my, my," Valentine said, and shook her head.
Even skimming the surface of Eddie's thoughts left her
feeling in need of a brain shampoo. She wondered who
the young vampire harassing him was, and what the
conversation was about. "Something *fraught*," she complained. "The whole damn town's full of fraught.
Should have stayed in L.A."

Not only fraught, but the Scrolls of Silk were in the
mix as well. Which meant the woman's agenda was po-
litical, and extremely anti-Nighthawk. The scrolls were
a Goddess-damned nuisance, and no matter how many
times the Enforcers destroyed what was supposed to be
the last existing copy of the thing, another copy eventually cropped up. Some things were best forgotten. Some
books were best burned. The Scrolls ranked up there
with the Protocols of the Elders of Zion as sicko propaganda best kept from the world. In the case of the
Scrolls, the purpose wasn't anti-Semitism as it was in
the Protocols, but vicious accusations against the
Nighthawk line.

It was all that hotel's fault, she decided. Call a place
the Silk Road, capitalize, even indirectly, on vampire
mystique, and weird things were bound to happen.
Somebody ought to do something about it, she thought.
Then Valentine got dressed, combed out her long black
curls, carefully applied very red lipstick, and went to the
party.

* * *

"You're pacing."

Haven stood still long enough to look at Char. "So are you."

He was wearing a suit, an expensive, well-tailored suit Char had picked out for him. She'd suggested the shoes, the shirt, and the tie as well. Haven didn't mind her choices since he didn't care much about clothes. Char didn't care much about clothes either, but she looked good in what she was wearing. For once she wasn't in black, but a floaty blue and white print dress. The spaghetti straps showed off her buff shoulders and arms. He would have liked the skirt to be shorter, to show off her legs. He guessed a certain amount of modesty was suitable for a wedding.

The room was full of roses, lilies, and orchids arranged in tall crystal vases. The floor was shining white marble; the walls were hung with palest pink watered-silk drapes. A fountain burbled gently in the center of the room. It was all very tasteful, feminine, and romantic, Haven supposed. This wasn't even the wedding chapel but a reception area. The chapel was through an arched doorway on the other side of the reception room. The staff was discreetly out of sight since welcoming them, and hopefully wouldn't reappear until the happy couple put in an appearance.

"Are we early or are they late?" he asked. "Think we should have picked them up at their hotel?"

"I'm nervous," she said, and went back to pacing.

Haven wasn't sure she'd heard his questions. Char

was definitely distracted. So was he, but he made himself stay still. "Me too."

"You what?"

"Nervous."

"Why?"

Haven wasn't prepared to tell her yet. Not here. Way too public. And he had to be very careful in how he told his Enforcer lover what he knew and how he knew it.

He glanced toward a side table, where bottles chilled in ice buckets. "Maybe we should break into the champagne."

"Jebel!"

He expected the reaction, and chuckled. "If you're hungry, there's a cake too."

He'd thought about telling Char about Martina when she first woke up. But the look in her eyes was haunted when she opened them. She told him she'd had daymares before he could ask what was wrong. Then she'd grabbed him and made love to him and he hadn't minded that a bit. It distracted both of them, and left no time for conversation before they had to get dressed for the wedding.

"Isn't this place a little too classy?" Haven asked. "For Santini."

"Definitely too classy for Santini, but not for Della. Were you expecting them to be married by an Elvis impersonator?"

"Yeah."

"She wanted to get married at the Venetian," Char told him. "The thought of that much opulence scared

Santini to death. They compromised on a nice wedding chapel."

"Della runs a homeless shelter. I didn't expect she'd want anything fancy."

"You don't know Della. Not the Della I knew back in Seattle. Back when we shared a nest with—" Char shook her head.

She didn't have to say it, and he didn't have to be a mind reader to know what she was thinking. Who. Jimmy Bluecorn. The sacred, the beloved, the vampire who'd made her. Haven almost growled at the thought, both with jealousy and the lingering perception that it was wrong to make anyone a vampire. Char had been a volunteer, he reminded himself. Vampire laws allowed a vampire to take whoever they wanted without asking permission, but apparently the sacred Jimmy Bluecorn wasn't that kind of a guy. He was so perfect and blessed of memory that Char wasn't over him yet. And vampire laws stated that once you were made into a vampire, you severed all ties with your bloodparent. Char had issues 'cause she still had the hots for good old Jimmy.

"It's hero worship," she said, picking up on Haven's resentment. "Don't you ever think it's any more than that."

"That's bullshit," he answered, but he smiled when he said it.

Char appreciated the effort it took Jebel to make light of something he saw as a threat to their relationship. Which was ironic, because she was well aware of how ambivalent he remained about being involved with a vampire. She had her problems, he had his. "We make it work," she said, discovering that they were staring into each other's eyes and wondering how long this had been going on.

He nodded. "I don't know how."

Desire sang between them. "That's how." Lust sent heat through her, set her fangs aching, but she made herself turn away. She felt his disappointment, and said, "A wedding chapel isn't the place for what we have in mind."

"If the bride and groom are going to be late—"

"Snogging in the chapel is not a good way to fill in the time."

"Snogging? What the hell's—"

"It's a British term."

"You want to do it on the altar?"

Char couldn't repress a laugh at the images this suggestion invoked. "You are not that kinky, Jebel. I am," she added, and felt her rough man's grin of disbelief. "But you like to think I'm a lady."

"I know you're a lady."

She walked across the reception area and peered into the chapel. "Besides, there isn't an altar."

She could tell there was something on his mind besides sex. He was concerned, and it went deeper than nerves about being best man at a wedding. Her concern went deeper than being the maid of honor.

As for that, Char found it odd that Della had asked her since they'd never exactly been close. What was even odder was that a companion had survived the death of her vampire lover and recovered enough sanity and self to fall in love with another mortal. Who knew such a thing could happen? There was nothing in the Laws of the Blood that forbade this union. Of course, the Laws were written for and by vampires. Since companions and slaves existed only in relation to their masters, very little attention was paid to the mortal members of the underneath world.

There weren't many Laws specifically aimed at Nighthawks, either. The Laws that applied to all vampires applied to those who enforced the Laws as well. Only, there were traditions among Enforcers, unwritten Laws, codes of behavior. She wasn't sure if she'd violated the codes last day, or if something else was going on. She hoped her dilemma was as simple as being rude for not having introduced herself to the Enforcer of the City when he saved her from burning to a crisp inside her own daymare.

It probably wasn't that simple, of course. The situations the psychically gifted got themselves into were rarely simple. Instead of coincidences, her kind had to deal with synchronicity. People met for reasons, complex, obscure, and dangerous. It was all very—

"Fraught," she muttered, and wondered why she'd chosen that word as a finger of ice ran up her spine.

"What?" Jebel asked.

"Nothing."

Even as she answered him, she almost forgot Jebel's presence. Her mind filled with the image of the Nighthawk she'd met above Las Vegas—inside her head—wherever. Inside both their dreams was the appropriate site where they'd met, she supposed, though it had felt very much as though they were out in the real daylight world. The connection was almost too complex to comprehend, too big to take in. The magic involved had been draining, and exhilarating.

She'd woken up so hungry she'd very nearly drained Jebel of every drop of blood in him. She hadn't bitten him, had she? Surely she'd remember that. And he'd have mentioned it. She was still horny even though Jebel never failed to satisfy her physical needs. Most of them.

"I'm going to have to bite you soon," she said. She turned back to him. His expression was neutral, but at least the look in his eyes was curious rather than wary.

"You're hungry," he said. He nodded. "I understand." He gestured toward the chapel. "Marry me first."

To her shock, Char realized Jebel Haven was completely serious. "We can't. Don't—"

"Until death do we part."

"Until rebirth do we part," she countered. Was he calling her bluff somehow? Putting another obstacle in the way between his veins and her needs? He sounded, looked, and felt dead serious.

"Why not get married?" he asked. "It's not against the Laws, is it?"

"Birth certificates," she said. "Blood tests."

"Can be gotten around."

"Outstanding warrants," Char reminded him. "Yours."

"I have fake IDs."

"Wouldn't that make it a fake marriage?"

"Not if we mean it."

This left Char with her mouth hanging open, and feeling like warm butter was flowing through her veins. It melted her. Even though some small part of her protested that she was a stern, fearsome creature of the night and such sloppy emotions should be alien, she couldn't help but smile at the mortal who had once filled her full of shotgun pellets. He'd thought she was a murderous werewolf at the time. She'd been under orders to kill him.

"To think it's come to this," she said, and started toward him.

But the door opened before she reached Jebel, and they both turned at the sound. The bride and groom had not arrived. A vampire stood in the doorway instead, a tall, broad-shouldered male, dark-haired, dressed in black, wearing sunglasses.

Char gasped. "You!" she said, with embarrassing shrillness in her tone.

Jebel picked up on her distress and reached inside his jacket. Of course, Jebel was wearing a weapon to a wedding. Her mortal was still a shoot-first-why-bother-with-questions sort of man.

The vampire noticed, and moved.

Char put herself between Jebel and the newcomer. She saw a flash of claw, heard a gun being drawn. "Don't!" she ordered both of them.

Both stopped at the crack of power in her voice. Tense stillness settled over the room. *Who are you?*

What are you doing here? She screamed the thoughts at the vampire—the Nighthawk.

The other vampire—slowly—held a hand up, a conciliatory gesture. His claws were retracted. "I'm here for—"

"Geoff?" Della's voice cut across the other Nighthawk's words. They all turned their attention to the newly arrived bride, who stood between Santini and Baker in the entrance. Della was smiling as she peered curiously at the newcomer. "Geoff?" she repeated.

At first Geoff Sterling didn't recognize the mortal woman dressed in bridal satin and lace, but her voice was very familiar. He took off the sunglasses to get a better look. He noted that the bride was not wearing white, but silver. Silver seemed appropriate. She'd prefer platinum, he thought, and then remembered who she was. Della. Krystalle's companion. But Krystalle was long dead. Why was Della still alive if her mistress was dead? And what was she doing in a Las Vegas wedding chapel? Okay, that was obvious. But what was Della's connection to the other Nighthawk? He cast a quick glance at the Nighthawk—the one wearing the floaty blue and white dress. A vampire bridal attendant? It was all very confusing.

There were three mortal men in the room. Their hostile looks told him they knew what he was, and were not happy about it. None of them were companions, or even slaves. Geoff made himself smile. Better to make peace now, and ask questions later.

He held his hands out to Della. He said, "I didn't want to miss your wedding."

"Who is he?" the mortal behind him spoke, voice rough, deep, and very suspicious.

"I have n—" the Nighthawk began.

"I'm from the old nest in Seattle," Geoff cut in over the suspicion.

"He was Jimmy Bluecorn's companion after you," Della explained to the other vampire.

For some reason the tension in the room only grew at this information. Geoff ignored it, and added, "And I'm here to give the bride away."

Chapter 8

"WAS YOUR, UH, friend, really going to try to shoot me?" Geoff asked Charlotte McCairn.

They hadn't been formally introduced, but he knew her name. Jimmy had talked about her. Now that the wedding was over and they were back in the reception room for cake and champagne, Geoff finally had the chance to talk to Charlotte. They were on the opposite side of the room from the mortals, near the building entrance. Geoff noticed that Charlotte made sure that she was between him and the others. He admired her protective instincts. He'd heard a lot of good things about her.

In his early days as Jimmy Bluecorn's companion, Geoff had been jealous of the woman he'd replaced. That she'd gone on to be a vampire he knew, of course. He hadn't known she'd also made the transition to Nighthawk. Not being in the Enforcer loop, there was a lot he didn't need or want to know. He did want to know about Charlotte, and her motley group of mortals.

"He wouldn't have *tried* to shoot you," she answered Geoff's question after she took a sip of champagne. "The bullet wound wouldn't have killed you, of course, but the considerable pain from the explosive charge would have slowed you down."

She sounded quite pleased at the knowledge that a mortal was capable of inflicting pain on a vampire.

"How did he know what I am? Why would he want to shoot me?"

"Instinct," she replied. "To protect me."

"He belongs to you." Not a question.

"Yes." Said with pride. And the unspoken assertion that she belonged to the mortal as well. With the threat that she protected what was hers underlying everything else.

This was not possible. It was not right. He gestured toward the table, where the mortals gathered around the wedding cake. The bride and groom had their heads together, oblivious of everyone else. Charlotte's mortal and the large African-American male were carefully watching him and Charlotte. The black man was openly hostile. The man who was a lover if not a companion didn't look friendly, but there was a wait-and-see attitude about him. Vampires obviously didn't scare him.

"He doesn't have a chance against me," Geoff said.

Charlotte's smile was full of confidence. "But he doesn't know that."

Maybe it would be best to move on to something else. "Your friends," he began. "Aren't there Laws—"

"Are you the Enforcer of the City?"

She had a tight shield around her thoughts, but nerves underlay her sharp tone.

"Of course not," he answered. "I'm not from around here."

"But you are an Enforcer."

He deliberately kept very calm. "I'm a Nighthawk. Just like you. You're not the Enforcer of the City, either. Are you?"

"That's irrelevant," she said. But she was thinking, *If I'm not, and you're not, then who is?*

Does it matter?

Of course it matters! She was sure it mattered. If there were two other Nighthawks in town, surely the Enforcer of the City was going to notice something different in the psychic makeup of the area. And surely the Enforcer was going to want to know why, and come looking. Char decided that maybe it would be best if she came up with an innocuous explanation and presented it to the Enforcer first. "We're supposed to contact the Enforcer when we enter their territory," she reminded the other Nighthawk. "I'm here on vacation myself."

"You need to practice that line some more," Geoff answered. He took a sip of champagne. "Me, I'm here on business."

"What kind of business?" she immediately wanted to know.

"You have a suspicious nature."

"I am an Enforcer."

"I'm not."

Char blinked, and took a few deep breaths. She'd been trained as an Enforcer by Marguerite of Portland. She worked for Istvan, the Enforcer they called in for the really dangerous jobs. While she was more a researcher than a field op, and had bent a few Laws herself in keeping Haven rather than killing him, she was still a member of the Enforcer organization. All right, she was bending custom if not the Law now by not mentioning her presence to Las Vegas's official Enforcer. But bending wasn't the same as *breaking* the Law.

"You're hyperventilating," Sterling said. He was smiling quite cheerfully. "Does the idea of a non-Enforcer Nighthawk upset you that much?"

She waved her hand at him, and looked around almost nervously. "Shhh. You shouldn't talk about that. You shouldn't admit to it." Her nerves turned into an angry glare. "In fact, you shouldn't *be*. Who made you? Why haven't you—?"

"Long story," he cut her off. "My story."

"It isn't allowed."

"It's a free country. I don't have to go into the family business if I don't want to."

"Free—? How can you say we're free? We have obligations." Char realized she was sputtering with indignation, and hated the way Geoff Sterling simply stood there and looked at her. "Stop being so condescending."

"I haven't said a thing."

"Your eyes were laughing."

He put a hand over his heart. "You wound me."

"I might," she threatened.

A flicker of fire in his eyes reminded her they were vampires. "Do you really want to hurt me?" The challenge was there, under the mock hurt in his voice. He took a small step closer to her. "Of course, a bit of mutual hunting might be fun."

She shook her head. "No. I didn't mean—"

"You did. The Heart of the Hunter is the greatest prize. Isn't that how the saying goes? Hasn't the Council decreed that all Nighthawks must serve them? Isn't it a killing offense not to comply?" He glanced toward Jebel and the rest of the mortals. Whether it was a threat against her friends, or a reminder of the irregularities in her own life, she wasn't sure. "You going to report me?"

She was glad he didn't ask if she was going to hunt him. As far as she knew, no Nighthawk had ever killed another Nighthawk. She wasn't even sure it could be done, and she'd researched everything she could about vampires. A *dhamphir* could do it. Istvan, the Enforcer's Enforcer, was a *dhamphir.* If she reported Geoff Sterling's existence to Istvan—

But how could she rat out one of Jimmy Bluecorn's kids?

"You're having an ethical dilemma, aren't you?" He gently took the champagne glass from her hand and set both their glasses on the nearest table.

"How can you tell?" she asked when he turned back to her. "Is smoke coming out of my ears?"

"That was last day," he said, and took her by the arm.

"When I was on fire."

"When I saved your life."

"That was a dream."

"You didn't think so at the time." He moved with her toward the door.

She was aware of Jebel tensing behind her, but she could not take her attention away from Geoff Sterling. She didn't dare take her attention from him. He was a loose cannon. He had to be up to something. He put on his sunglasses.

"Let's go for a walk," he said.

"All right," she said, and went out with him into the night.

Baker put a hand on Haven's arm as he started to go after the vampires. "What's with that guy?" Baker asked. "I couldn't get near them. I couldn't hear them. Was he using some kind of vampire force field? Can they do that? Or was it your girlfriend?"

Haven shook off Baker's hand, but he turned to the other man rather than follow his impulse. "I don't know," was his answer to all Baker's questions.

Had Sterling exerted influence on them? Everyone in the room had psychic ability to one extent or another. Baker and Santini's gifts were very low level, but they had enough to be exploited by vampires.

"Della and Santini weren't paying attention to Char and Sterling. And I was being polite," Haven finally concluded.

"I wasn't," Baker answered. He put his big, broad frame in front of Haven. "What's Char doing with that vampire? Where are they going? Hunting?"

"She doesn't hunt humans," Haven reminded Baker. "You know that."

"Do I? Really? Do you?"

"The girl thinks she's a superhero, a protector of humanity. Why won't you get that through your head?"

"My head's on right, yours never has been. And you've gotten worse since you started fucking the dead."

Haven didn't answer that crack. He did not want this confrontation, wasn't going to take any bait. Restraint from him? Who'd have thought it possible? Today he'd found out he needed to protect Char from vampires. He hated the thought of having to protect her from one of the few humans he called friend. There was no question he'd take out Baker if he had to, but he didn't want to. He didn't want to think about it.

And where was Char when he was faced with a pair of crises? Off somewhere with another vampire, a Hollywood-handsome, smooth-as-silk, way-too-full-of-himself asshole who had a look in his eye Haven definitely didn't like.

It was a good thing for everyone involved that vampires didn't fuck each other. If they did, Haven would let himself be more jealous than concerned about Char going off with the stranger.

"I still don't like it."

"I don't like anything about this trip," Baker said.

Haven wondered where the vampires were going, and only one place occurred to him. He'd been planning on checking the place out anyway. And Char might need backup if she went in there. Shit! She didn't know about the vampire plot against the Enforcers.

"You thirsty?" he asked Baker.

Baker still looked pissed off, but he nodded curtly. Making the assumption that Haven was up to something, he abandoned the argument. "Champagne's never been my drink."

"Good. Let's drop the bride and groom off at their hotel, then head for a bar at the Silk Road."

The bar was called the Caravanserai, of course. Three steps and a half-circle of arches and pillars separated it from the casino floor. A fountain played in the middle of the room, the tinkling of water counterpoint to the song of the slot machines not too far away. The Caravanserai was decorated in blue and white tile and Persian rugs, the tables were low, carved, and inlaid, with colorful cushions piled around them rather than chairs. The cocktail waitresses were dressed in short, clinging red silk costumes, with silver belts and anklets that jingled when they moved.

At this time of night the bartenders on duty were usually a pair of vampires, but Ben noticed that mortals had taken the late shift tonight. Martina's nest was slacking off. Ben didn't really mind, as he didn't want to be around any of her crew. Maybe he'd complain to Ibis about it. Or maybe he'd let it go, since this might not be a good time to have the ancient vampire's attention on him.

He sat with his back to the wall and a clear view of the entrance and took a good look around the place, all out of long habit. There were a few empty tables, but business was all right. No one had noticed him enter, and the mortal tourists paid him no mind as he sat nursing a drink made of Kahlúa and strong coffee. There was a certain amount of psychic energy in the room, normal, low-level stuff. Any crowd had a few with the gift, but Ben felt no indication that anyone in the place had ever tasted a drop of vampire blood.

No spies, he decided. No one watching. He didn't expect any, but he'd found in his mortal life that paranoia was a good trait to cultivate. He liked to keep his business private.

He placed several objects on the shining tiles of the table, and waited. It wasn't long before he felt Reese approaching. Keeping his gaze on the large red stone, Ben allowed anticipation to build as the fireball of magical energy grew closer. He didn't look up until Morgan Reese was at the entrance.

Though he was nearly blinded by the glow of psychic power, Ben didn't see Reese immediately. A pair of men entered the bar first, one black, one white, both large, blocking the sight of the smaller man. Reese was only a step behind, and when the two men moved aside to find a table for themselves, they seemed to take some of the energy with them. Ben frowned at this, but quickly forgot the mortals, concentrating on Reese as the magician came up to the table.

He gestured for Reese to have a seat.

Reese gave Ben a moment of stubborn resistance, then settled down on a cushion. "This place is stupid," Reese announced. "If you're going to keep forcing me to meet you, pick some place with chairs next time."

"Fair enough." Ben waved over a waitress, and waited for Reese to order before he pushed what he'd brought toward the magician. There was the faceted red stone the size of an egg, a gold chalice etched with strange symbols, and a blue three-ring binder. "Presents."

Reese gave a sneering glance at the stone and the cup. "I can get these in the gift shop."

Ben smiled. "Touch them, then tell me you can."

Reese put a hand out, and a pulse of energy spread out in a hot wave from the ruby even before he touched it. Reese pulled his hand back.

Nearby, someone said, "Holy fucking shit!"

Ben chuckled, agreeing with the assessment of the unfortunate tourist who had enough talent to feel the power surge. "Real magic," he whispered to Reese, leaning closer to the magician. "Real artifacts. Real tools."

Shock, pleasure, greed all washed through Reese. He looked at Ben with shining eyes. "Implements for performing ritual magic. From the museum." Ben nodded. "For me. You're giving them to me."

There was no surprise in his tone, and very little gratitude. Morgan Reese believed that he deserved everything, and Ben agreed with him. He would give Reese everything, because Reese belonged to him.

"Power is for taking," Ben told Reese. "For using."

Reese nodded, then he finally looked at the binder. "What's in the book?"

Chapter 9

"WHERE ARE WE going?"

Geoff Sterling answered her question with one of his own. "Where do you want to go?"

"The Silk Road, of course. But . . ." Char looked around nervously.

She half expected the Enforcer of the City to step out of the shadows and demand to know what they were doing here. Overhead the stars didn't have a chance of showing against all the light thrown up by the city. But a nearly full moon was out, shining down on the tower of the nearby Stratosphere. Heavy traffic moved in the street, though the sidewalk where they stood was relatively empty. Wedding chapels lined the street, lights and music and joy spilling out from many of them.

"Romantic place," Sterling said. "Let's get out of

here. Why the Silk Road?" he asked as they began to walk.

Char wished she wasn't wearing high-heeled shoes. Not that they hurt the tough skin of her feet—vampires didn't get blisters—but she wasn't used to walking in anything that tilted her legs and hips at such an awkward angle. It'd been a while since she'd done the girly girl thing. Jimmy Bluecorn liked her in spiked heels and short skirts, back in the '80s when they went to a lot of Heavy Metal concerts. She missed the '80s, but not the shoes.

"Why the Silk Road?" she replied to Sterling's question. "To check out the casino, of course."

Sterling took her hand in his as they walked, and for some reason, Char let him. "You don't seem the gambling type."

"To check out my investment, then."

"You too, huh?"

"Well, no, actually." She was, she knew, an inveterate truth teller. "I heard about the investment opportunity, but—"

"You don't earn much on an Enforcer's salary," Sterling finished for her.

"If you were an Enforcer," she informed him, "you would know that one does not actually get paid for serving and protecting the community."

"Except in fresh corpses."

Char looked around, though she didn't really expect them to be overheard. "Yeah."

"Go on," he urged. "Tell me more about the Silk

Road. Is that where you were trying to get last day?" he added. "Or were you just trying to fly into the sun?"

"Speaking of the sun," she asked, "why are you wearing shades right now?"

"I'm from L.A.," he answered. "Even worse, I'm from Hollywood."

"That's where you went, after you left Seattle?"

"Where'd you go?" he countered. "After you left Seattle?"

He hadn't answered her question about the sunglasses, but she answered him. "Portland first. Now I live in Arizona."

"And you're in Las Vegas for the wedding. Only for the wedding?"

"And you're in Las Vegas for what? The film exhibitors' convention?" she said. "I remember hearing about that. Are you really in the movies?"

"Production," he said. "My partner and I have done a couple of projects. You see *If Truth Be Told*? That's one of ours."

"I've seen it." She hated to admit it, but like most vampires, she loved vampire movies. They were the ultimate guilty pleasure. It was rather delicious to think that a vampire had produced a vampire film. "It was a terrible movie," she added.

"I know. Straight to video. It would have been great if Selim had let us use the original script. But no, he had to protect his ass."

"You know Selim? The Enforcer of Los Angeles? Selim knows there's a rogue Nighthawk in his city?"

Her shock made him laugh. "Girl, you are so cute."

She suspected that by cute, he meant naïve. Fine. He could believe that if he wanted to. To pull her hand away from his would have been petulant.

"Selim takes good care of his city," Sterling assured her. "If it makes you feel any better about me, I'll admit that I did help him thin an overpopulation of strigs a while back. He knows all I want is to be left alone."

Okay, she'd buy Sterling's explanations for now, and check with Selim when she got back home. Sterling still had no business being an undeclared Nighthawk. She was very far from knowing what she should do about it. She wasn't exactly the most action-oriented queen of the night.

"I do research," she said. "That's the real reason I want to go to the Silk Road."

"Going to waltz in and ask to look in the vault?"

"Of course not!" She gave him a hard look. "You know about the vault? You're interested in the old knowledge?"

"I've heard the rumors."

"And what do you think of them?"

"That it all sounds too good to be true. I wonder who started the rumors. And why. We're a secretive culture. It seems very unlikely that someone would store all our secrets in one place, and then a rumor of the storage place would start to circulate in the underground gossip mills. Sounds like a trap to me."

"Me too," she agreed. Too quickly. And she wished

she'd bit her tongue before she said anything. Vampires were supposed to be secretive! It was a survival skill she'd yet to learn. "I also wonder why the Council allowed the owner to use the Silk Road theme."

"Why do you think, Hunter?"

"Because the Council doesn't get out much," she suggested. "Besides, an exotic lost city theme certainly suits a Las Vegas hotel. And most of our kind don't know about the city. Not that most strigoi would be interested, of course. Most of them have no interest in history. Most have no interest in magic other than knowing the spell to turn a companion."

"Enforcers have encouraged this lack of interest, haven't they?"

While his tone was not exactly accusatory, it was heavy on sarcasm. While she chose not to answer this, they reached a corner. Geoff turned them left and they crossed, cutting easily through the heavy traffic. Char reflected that she probably would have waited at the crosswalk for a green light even though she had no need for such mundanely mortal behavior.

"Maybe you hang with mortals too much," Sterling observed.

She didn't answer this comment, either, but she did ask, "You have a destination in mind?" when they reached the other side of the street.

"Yes." They walked another block, then he paused.

Char was aware of his intensity, then of what he was searching for. "Vampires."

"Not very far away. Come on."

When he would have led her on, Char balked. "Why? You aren't looking for a snack, are you?"

He laughed. "You get a mental sniff of that bunch? Carrion."

"Light addicts," she corrected. "It's an illness. We should—"

"Feel sorry for them?"

"Avoid them," she answered. "Honey, I'm not that politically correct."

The grin he flashed at her held a hint of mating fang. "You called me honey."

She jerked her hand from his. "Don't take it personally."

"Of course not," he said. He started off down the street once more. "You coming?" he called back when she hesitated to follow.

She thought about finding Jebel. She thought about her longing to visit the Silk Road. She recalled that Geoff Sterling was an unregistered Nighthawk. She wasn't yet sure what she needed to do about that, but letting him wander alone among the city's population of neon junkies didn't seem like the sort of thing a responsible Enforcer should do.

She caught up with him in a few steps. "What do you want with the junkies?"

He gave her a strange look. "Nothing."

The next block held the blank wall of a huge parking garage. Traffic was thin for the moment, and the only illumination was from streetlights on each corner. The heat of the day still pulsed from concrete and blacktop, but the darkness between the corners was cool and comforting to creatures of their kind. She let Geoff Sterling take her hand again, and that was cool too, and the pulse beneath smooth, dense flesh was slow, slow and steady.

Within a few moments they turned the corner, going from darkness into glaring, garish light. Before them stretched several long blocks of a street that had been turned into a pedestrian mall. The lights of some of the city's older casinos lit up both sides of the mall. A canopy of light and laser arched over the street, stretching for several blocks. Music blared from all around, the lights changing and pulsing with the songs.

"Fremont Street," he said, and she felt his pulse quicken.

"I've heard of it," she answered. "This area is called the Fremont Street Experience. Or neon junkie heaven."

The street was crowded with people, faces turned up to the lightshow. There were a lot of vampires in the crowd. Geoff Sterling walked into the crowd, bringing her with him, moving well up the street before coming to a stop.

He moved with solemn grace, like he was performing some sort of rite. Nervous energy that was close to fear radiated from him.

"Just remember that I saved your ass," he told her. Then he looked up, and took off his sunglasses.

As he took them off, Char realized why he'd been

wearing them. The light drew him, fascinated him, the way it did—

While Geoff turned his face to the moving, pulsing, beautiful lights, Char took a quick, hard look around. Even if she hadn't been able to recognize the distinct energy pattern that said vampire, she would have known which ones they were. Skinny as sticks, it was hard to tell male from female. They took a lot of blood before heading out to watch the lights, so they weren't as pale as normal strigoi. The blood made them high, made them more receptive to the thing that truly turned them on. Their age dragged on them, they wore it like heavy winter clothes, layer upon layer of years.

Sick, she thought. *Totally sick. Senile. Vampire Alzheimer's.*

She shuddered at the thought that she could ever be like that. Then she grew aware of the man beside her. His body was stiff with tension, his face turned up to the lights.

She shook him. "You're smiling," she told him, pitching her voice to reach him beneath the Jimi Hendrix song rolling over the street. "Just like the mortals all around you are smiling. You're not like them—the carrion." He'd been right to call the light addicts that. "Don't do this to yourself. You just like the lights. Geoff. Geoff!" She hit him on the shoulder. When a Nighthawk hits someone, even another Nighthawk, it has an effect.

Geoff jumped, shook himself, and looked away from the overhead lightshow, down at her. "What'd you do that for? I was enjoying—"

"You requested an ass saving, Mr. Sterling. This service has cheerfully been provided to you."

He laughed. "Free of charge?"

"No. I could use a cup of coffee."

"Coffee." He rubbed his jaw, and carefully put the sunglasses back on. "I don't think I want to be out here without these," he admitted. "I like the lights too much. Come on." He took her hand again as the lightshow faded from the overhead projectors. "I could use a cup of coffee too."

There were shops wedged in between casino entrances, and plenty of carts and kiosks in the street hawking everything a tourist could want. It wasn't long before they found a vendor selling pastries and coffee, both hot and cold.

When they got in line, Char wasn't surprised that there was a vampire waiting in front of them. Within a few moments she became aware of another one behind them. *How predictable,* she thought. *I bet most of this place's business is from us.*

"I won't be surprised if the vendor is one of us," Geoff answered her thought.

"Me, either," said the vampire woman behind them.

While Char didn't mind that Geoff Sterling picked up her surface thoughts, Char turned around angrily to face the woman who'd rudely intruded.

"Hi, Val," Geoff greeted the woman before Char could say anything. "You didn't go to the party."

"I went," this Val person answered. She gave Geoff a vaguely annoyed look. "You didn't."

He made a dismissive gesture. "And we're both here now. Charlotte McCairn," he said. "Meet my business partner, Valentine."

Char was stunned, though she didn't know why. He hadn't said he worked with a companion or slaves. Why not go into business with another vampire? This also brought into doubt her assumption about his being a strig. "You two share a nest?"

Valentine regarded Char out of huge, dark eyes. There was humor in those eyes, and lots and lots of secrets. This vampire friend of Geoff's was very old, Char realized. Small, beautiful, and—

"Built like a brick shithouse," Valentine supplied.

"I wasn't thinking that," Char answered quickly. It was hard not to notice Valentine's figure in the skimpy little black dress she was wearing.

"Jealous?" Geoff asked.

"Of what?" Char demanded. "I'm not so bad loo—"

"That wasn't what I meant." The way he looked her over was very disconcerting. So disconcerting that her claws and fangs started to come out.

"Not here, children." Valentine's hand landed on Char's shoulder, sending a comforting warmth like nothing she'd ever felt before through Char. "She's blushing, Geoffrey," Valentine said. "Don't tease. Go get us some coffee," she added. She pointed toward a row of benches in the center of the street. "We'll be waiting over there."

Char realized the three of them had moved out of the line when Geoff dutifully returned to waiting. And she dutifully accompanied Valentine through the tourist crowd to the benches. Valentine's attention was drawn to the crowd after they were seated. The mortals passing by took no notice of them as they strolled and shopped, waiting for the light and music show overhead to begin again. The vampires intent on their own wait paid them even less attention.

"You're here looking for someone," Char concluded. "Not Geoff."

Valentine sighed. "So I am. Don't know why I'm bothering. You haven't seen Duke around, have you?"

"I don't know what he looks like."

Valentine gave her a sideways look. "You know a Nighthawk when you see one?"

Geoff joined them before Char could answer. He held a tall paper cup in each hand. Char was distracted by the fresh-brewed scent. He handed one of the cups to her.

"Keep it," Valentine said when Geoff turned to her. "Have a seat." She took a cell phone out of her purse as Geoff sat down. She punched numbers, waited, then said, "It's me. What do you mean how'd *I* get your number? Thought you'd like to know that there may be a situation, and the local boy doesn't seem to be around. You know the new hotel in town? Think there might be some trouble because of it. I'll call you back."

Char strained to hear the voice on the other side of the conversation, but could not make anything out before Valentine turned off the phone and put it away. Valentine glanced at Char and Geoff. "She wants me to call her on a landline."

"Who?" they both asked.

All of Char's psychic warning bells were going off. "What's going on? Who are you?"

Valentine seemed to have forgotten them for the moment. She looked at the passing people with wide, frightened eyes. Char could feel the woman's fear of the crowd like a weight on her own chest.

"I don't want to be here," Valentine said. "Too much. Too open."

"Stop it, Val." Geoff spoke loudly and harshly. "Keep it together. If you're involved in something, you can't make excuses."

Valentine took a few deep breaths, then turned a glare on Geoff. "I hate you."

He smiled. "Good. What's up?"

Char recognized Valentine's problem, and was not sure she approved of Sterling's lack of sympathy for his partner's fear of crowds. But from his own gesture of making himself stare into the most intent lights he could find, she supposed his approach to therapy was a brutally direct one.

Valentine drained Geoff's cup of scalding coffee before she answered. "I'm looking for Eddie," she said, and got to her feet. "He'll know what's up."

Geoff got up, and Char stood as well. She was totally confused, but felt she needed to do something, something official and Enforcer-like. But what the hell was the crisis?

"What do you want with Eddie?" Geoff asked.

"How can we help?" Char asked Valentine.

"We?"

"You two can look for the Scrolls of Silk," Valentine answered. She turned away, then paused and looked over her shoulder. "But don't read them," she ordered. "They'll make you go blind."

Then she disappeared. Not only did Valentine wrap the few shadows that existed in the brightly lit area around her, she vanished so quickly and completely that Char couldn't feel even the residue of Valentine's passing.

She gaped at Geoff. "Who is she?"

"You don't want to know," he answered.

"What are the Scrolls of Silk?"

He held his hand out to her again. "Let's go find out, shall we?"

Chapter 10

CHAR CAME IN late, way late. Just before dawn. Haven felt her exhaustion and worry, even through his own troubles. She fell into bed beside him, and into the vampire death trance before Haven had a chance to struggle to a sitting position so he could talk to her. He cursed dawn for robbing him of his chance. Then closed his eyes again on a moan. Char lay beside him, stiff as stone, skin growing cold, in a place where he could do nothing to warn her. He feared he was too weak to help her.

He'd been in their hotel room for hours, nursing a headache like nothing he'd ever felt before. He'd been passing out, waking up, throwing up, and passing out again since Baker helped him out of the Silk Road bar and back to the hotel. The only reason he kept fighting back to consciousness was because he needed to tell

Char what had happened. Only after a while memory began to fade against the fierce onslaught of the pain.

There was nothing he could do for now but rest, stop fighting the darkness. Char couldn't fight the dark; maybe he needed the same kind of rest she did. He'd been assaulted by one hell of a burst of magic. Magic made Char what she was. Maybe he'd had a dose of the same stuff. Like radiation poisoning.

"Magic," he mumbled, and fumbled to find her. It took so much work to roll over and wrap his arms around her stiff, still form. He wasn't sure if he was trying to protect her or draw comfort from knowing she was there with him. He did let the darkness take him, and couldn't remember how long it had been since he'd last slept even as he fell asleep.

The dream was a real ball buster, so bad that Haven woke up screaming. He cut the sound off fast enough when he jerked to a sitting position. He wasn't surprised when the hangover from hell hit him, and he almost welcomed the pain. It didn't hurt as much as the torture in the dream. In the dream he'd been burning, fire eating through him, frying away skin and muscle, burrowing into bone. God, it hurt!

The headache pounded and pulsed in his temples, but it was simple, ordinary pain. It was residue from a burst of magic, but that was ordinary for his world. He gave a quick glance down at the statue that would be his girl-friend in a few hours, patted her unfeeling rump, then went to down aspirin, a glass of whiskey, and take a quick shower. This treatment helped enough to get him functional.

Once dressed, he was reluctant to head back to the Silk Road. After last night the place scared him. The fear, more than anything else, even more than curiosity or the need to protect his lover, was what got him going. There was nothing from hell that Jebel Haven couldn't face down.

The way he figured it, the more demons he dealt with now, the less he'd have to deal with when he landed in the fiery pit.

Which brought back memory of the dream so vivid it made him shudder. He hoped to God it was a dream. Now that was a crazy thought, but what had happened was crazy. And that red stone—fire red and blood red—

He reached the elevator and paused until he forced the thoughts down and out of the moment.

Clare Murphy was waiting for him at the lobby entrance. She handed him a badge with his name on it.

"All-access pass?" Haven asked, clipping the badge onto his jacket collar.

"Something like that. It's coded to let you into any area I have access to."

Haven tilted his head to one side and gave the woman a not altogether teasing smile. "Does that include the money vault?"

"Ben wouldn't approve of that," was the companion's answer.

Haven considered pointing out that revolutions, even revolutions against creatures of the night, required a certain amount of financing. He let it go. Better to concentrate on the help the woman wanted and could give to the cause.

"Let me give you the tour," she said, and led him into the lobby.

"I need some information," he said, but she ignored him.

Gesturing toward the painted ceiling several stories overhead, she said, "See the night sky motif? It's significant."

Haven looked up. The paint and lighting design gave the look of a very real, very starry night. The black eyes of security cameras also looked down out of this star-filled work of art, but that was a normal part of all Las Vegas décor. It wasn't the security she was warning him about, but some vampire thing.

"I already know the interior design of this place is supposed to reflect an eternal summer night at a desert oasis. I've read the brochures." When she gave him an impatient look, he gave in and asked, "What's the significance?"

Murphy looked pleased, in the same way Char did when he fell for a question that led to an hour's worth of geekspeak answer.

"Rumor has it," she told him, "that the lobby ceiling was designed to exactly duplicate the positions of the stars the night the vampire city was destroyed."

"Yeah. So?"

"Meaning that the exact location of the ruins of the city can be determined by studying this star chart."

She seemed so pleased to be passing on this information that Haven held back any sarcastic comments about why anyone would care about finding the lost city. He supposed Char would care. He also didn't point out that he doubted this rumor. Vampires did not go around dropping clues to their existence. "It's not smart," he muttered. "Not safe."

She nodded. "I know. Come see the museum," she said, as though refuting this last thought.

"Fine." The quicker they got the tour over with, the sooner they could get to things he wanted to discuss.

They crossed the lobby, went down a wide hallway, and climbed up a grand staircase to where a line of people waited to go through a pair of gold doors. Murphy took him around the line, around a corner, and used her key card to open a door into a small room full of monitors and other security equipment. A pair of uniformed guards were in the room, their attention on the screens and boards. Only one of them looked away from the job when Murphy brought Haven inside.

The guard watched the door until Murphy secured it once more. Then he looked at Haven while he asked Murphy, "What's up, boss?"

"These are members of Ben's nest," Murphy told Haven instead of answering the guard. "Only underneath people work this room. We're going into the exhibit," she told her underling.

The guard took his attention off them as Murphy spoke. The pair were slaves, Haven guessed, who knew to mind their own business around their betters. Haven's skin crawled at this example of the vampire way of life and he momentarily wondered why he was looking to protect the Nighthawks from attack by another bunch of bloodsuckers.

Char, he reminded himself. Only for Char. And oh, yeah, the possibility that he might end up a Nighthawk himself.

Murphy took him through another door on the other side of the security station, and Haven noted how this door disappeared against the wall once it was closed.

"The place is full of hidden doors and corridors," Murphy said when she noticed him studying the spot where he knew the door was. She ran her hand along the wall. "Some of it's part of the hotel's theme. Mysterious secret corridors and treasure chambers and hidden gardens and stuff like that. There's a map to some of them on sale in the gift shops."

They kept their voices low, careful not to draw attention from the tourists filing by the nearby display cases.

"And the real secret chambers?" Haven asked.

"I know most of them."

"Vampires sleep in them."

"Some do. Most aren't that paranoid."

It was true that in this day and age most vampires only feared Enforcers, and then only if they trespassed against the numerous Laws.

"Martina's bunch hang out in the secret crypts?"

Murphy nodded. "Most of the time, yes."

"You know where they are?"

She nodded again. She held up a hand in warning. "They have their own separate alarm systems, and they have a group of slaves and companions specifically dedicated to protecting the nest members. Even if I could unlock all the doors for you, it'd still be hard to take them out in their sleep."

He gave a casual shrug. "Might be worth a shot."

"We want to protect the Nighthawks without giving ourselves away. Better if an Enforcer takes on the job."

"I could still take a look at their place."

"You could, but since none of Martina's vampires or their security mortals are sleeping in the vault today, any stray explosive stakes you might be carrying on your person won't have the chance to get buried in any vampires' hearts while you are *casually* having a look around."

Haven frowned at her easy reading of his intentions, and in disappointment at a missed opportunity. She gave a smug smile in response.

"Okay," he acknowledged. "No striking blows for the revolution just because I'm in a bad mood." After last night's meeting with the smug Geoff Sterling, the incident in the bar, and the bad dream, Haven was edgy. Killing a monster would help his mood. "If they're not at home today, where are they?" it finally occurred to him to ask.

"Don't know," Clare answered. "Yet. And I don't like it."

"Neither do I."

Not one bit. Maybe Martina's vampires were asleep. But what were their mortals up to? Was Char in danger of being discovered? His immediate impulse was to head back to their room to watch over her. His second impulse was to go hunting for Martina.

"What are you doing about it?" he asked Clare Murphy.

"I've got people trying to find them, but no luck so far. Martina has no right being out in the city," she went on. "It's Ben's territory. If Ben wasn't so involved with the new boy toy, he'd have told me to report Martina and her crew to the Enforcer's companion if I caught them being out after daylight."

Haven considered this for a moment, then said, "You called the Enforcer's companion without waiting for Ben's permission."

"Of course. Not that it's going to do any good." Her lips thinned to an angry line. "Damn Duke. He's useless—which I normally don't mind."

"Why won't it do any good? The local Enforcer ought to be the one to take this nest down."

"Duke let them build this place. He took their bribes. I don't know what he told the Council."

She gestured toward the display cases. Haven could feel the pulse of power in the room, like the vibrations of a huge engine. His headache was starting up again.

"Duke's useless," Murphy went on. "And now he's missing."

Haven's headache spiked on a surge of warning. "Missing?"

"Skipped town's my guess. His companion's frantic." Murphy moved away from the wall. "Let's get back to the tour. There's something I want you to see."

"Fine," Haven agreed between gritted teeth. He supposed he ought to get a look at this stuff. Maybe there was a weapon he could use in the piled-up magical clutter.

He thought she'd take him on a case-by-case tour of Ibis's magic shop, but instead she led him to one specific case. There were three objects inside. He recognized two of them. He could tell by only looking at it that the small gold ring with a carved carnelian scarab bezel was far heavier than it looked. It was ancient, and full of something.

"A soul was poured into it," he said. "Somehow."

"Yes," Murphy agreed. "That's what the announcer would say if you pushed the button on the case."

Okay, so he was picking up the magic vibes from an old ring. "Never mind. It's not important." He pointed at the gold cup—and the faceted red stone. "Those—"

"Yes?" Murphy urged quietly.

Haven looked around. Then hunched closer to the shorter woman to avoid anyone nearby overhearing. "They're fake."

"I know," she whispered back.

"I've seen them before," he told her. "The real ones. What are they?" He pointed at the red stone, remembering—"What is that?"

"It's called a dragon's egg," Murphy answered. "It's used in vampire alchemy, I think."

"Vampire alchemy?"

"Blood into gold instead of lead into gold, I guess. Maybe that's where they got the gold for the nest leaders' coins."

She thought. She guessed. "You don't really know what it's for."

"I know it's powerful. And—" Her mouth snapped closed and she shook her head.

Haven understood her sudden reaction. He took Murphy by the shoulders and turned her to face him. She was trembling. "You know Ben—your master, the master you told me you wanted to be on an equal footing with—he took the magical crap from the case. You want me to know, but you feel the need to defend Ben, too. It makes you crazy—the pull for freedom and the compulsion to protect twist at you all the time. It's okay." He was trying hard to act sane and reasonable, and it was really going against the grain.

He pulled the painfully confused companion into a momentary embrace. She pushed him away. She had to. After all, she *belonged* to Ben, but breathed a nearly silent, "Thanks," even as she stepped back.

"It's okay," he assured her. "You're not ratting out Ben. I saw him with the stuff."

She wiped a thin film of sweat off her forehead. "You know what Ben did?"

"Saw him give it to his new boyfriend. Right here in the hotel bar. Felt it," Haven added. "The witch boy made the rock—radiate?—just by passing his hand over it. Didn't you feel it, sometime around one?"

"I wasn't in the hotel after midnight last night." Murphy was visibly calmer now, her tone back to brisk and matter-of-fact. "Did you see what else Ben gave Morgan Reese?"

"A notebook, I think. I didn't get a very good look at it."

"It's the notebook that's important," she said. "The other stuff is toys."

"What's in the book?"

"Spells, of course. Ancient, powerful spells translated into English. Maybe even a translation of the Scrolls of Silk."

"The what?"

"Martina wants the information in the scrolls to hurt Enforcers. We need to get our hands on that book. Come with me."

She took him out of the treasure room, by the front entrance this time, and by back ways and private elevators to the heart of the hotel's security system. The control center contained walls of monitors, rows of sensor equipment. The place was manned by a couple dozen sharp-eyed, serious-looking people, all of them wearing headsets. No one gave him and Murphy more than a cursory glance as they moved through the room. Their eyes were on the gambling pits, the halls and lobby, the shops and pools, restaurants, bars, buffets, and every other public area of the hotel. One bank of screens showed more private areas of the Silk Road. This was the area where Murphy led Haven.

Murphy shooed the woman monitoring these screens away with a gesture. She took the woman's vacated chair, and gestured Haven to one next to it. As he sat, Murphy's fingers flew over a control panel, bringing up multiple views of the same scene.

"What am I looking at?" Haven asked, sweeping his gaze from screen to screen.

"Morgan Reese's dressing room."

She sounded grim and worried, Haven noted. This was obviously very important to her. He concentrated on the various views, trying to make out details before asking more questions. The space was large, full of all kinds of colorful junk—boxes and cabinets draped in bright satin cloths, even a guillotine and an ornately decorated animal cage. Typical stage magician stuff, Haven supposed. Another view showed a refrigerator and bar setup. Cameras covered several doors. There was a couch, a desk, several chairs.

A vampire was sleeping on the couch.

"Ben?"

"Ben," Murphy agreed. She was staring at views of the vampire, chewing a thumbnail worriedly. She obviously didn't like him being away from his usual safe sleeping place. "That's Reese," she said, pointing at the screens covering where the magician sat at a table.

Haven glanced at the man he'd seen in the bar last night, but his attention was inexorably drawn to the objects on the table. He couldn't bear to look at the red gem for more than a moment. It seemed bigger than he remembered. Even seeing it through the lens of a camera, it made his eyes burn and sent a wave of heat over his skin. The gold vessel didn't give off such nasty vibes.

"Look at him. Reese is reading the grimoire," Murphy said. "The translation of the scrolls is in there, along with a lot of potent spells."

Haven hung out with Char McCairn. He knew what a grimoire was. He recognized the blue plastic binder from seeing the vampire pass it to Reese in the bar last night. "That's the spell book, all right."

"We have to get it from Reese." She looked anxiously at her master, passed out on the couch. "We have to get Ben out of there."

"We?" Haven gave the woman a hard look. "You're head of security. Send a couple of your people to lug Benjy boy out."

She shot him a shocked look. "I can't do that!"

Haven shook his head in disgust. He glanced at the screens and back at the woman. The vampire on the couch didn't look to be in any danger. Reese's concentration was gleefully on the notebook, smiling and gesturing as he turned pages. "Ben wants to be in there, right?"

"Yes," the companion agreed reluctantly. "But the grimoire—"

"Nest politics is not my problem. I came here because of Martina, not to help you with your boyfriend's boyfriend. She's the problem. That's what you said yesterday." Haven got to his feet. "Now you don't even know where she is."

When he started to walk away, she asked, "Where are you going?"

"Looking for Duke," he answered. He glanced back at her briefly before he left. "You don't know where the city's Enforcer is. No Enforcer skips town without his companion. Doesn't that tell you something?"

Chapter 11

I USED TO be better at this.

I am good at it. Truth is, dreamriding looking for story ideas is a fun hobby. What I need to do now is going to lead to—implications.

Heads will roll. Hearts will be ripped out. I should call in the professionals. I called Olympias. She's the one with official sanction. Let her—

As if I trust Olympias to actually be of any help to anyone. It was cowardly of me to call her, even if I do hate getting involved. She might be a problem solver, but she's actually started believing the Council rules the strigoi race. Smart girl, but hard. Sorry I called her, even if the lost Enforcer does work for her.

Maybe he'll turn up. Maybe being out of the house is making me delusional.

Valentine let the thought and herself drift through

darkness. She could feel Geoff lying beside her. Not his frozen body, but sense the swirl of mental energy. His restlessness was distracting, but she fought the urge to intrude, to tell him to keep it down in there. The boy had his own searching to do, his own dreamriding to navigate. It wouldn't help if she deliberately distracted him.

She rather liked floating in this waking darkness, especially after the chaos of the night before. If she'd found Eddie for more than a few seconds of mental contact last night, she could stay inside herself now, rest and recover. But no, Eddie had to be elusive. And she had to have gotten distracted. Over and over again. She simply should not be allowed out alone in crowds. Geoff would say it was good for her, was always urging her to experience the world outside the walls of her home. What the hell did he know? What happened when a lurch of conscience sent her walking the streets last night? Did she find Eddie? No.

Shouldn't it have been the easiest thing in the world to find a vampire she'd made? Yes. Of course. She'd found three of them among the strigs wandering around staring at the pretty lights. It had been like a hot knife going through her heart every time she came across an old, discarded lover. Seeing them frightened her as well. Was it some weakness she'd passed to them that made them prey to the light sickness?

They got old, she told herself now. They never got new—never learned how to renew themselves with each new night. That's something we all have to cope with. Can't be taught. Can't be passed on. I hope.

Eddie may have become far too light-loving, but he wasn't helpless or harmless, Valentine would bet on that.

He's a rat, she remembered. He always has been. I was looking for a vampire when I should have been searching for a rat. Silly me.

I couldn't find him physically or mentally last night. I can't use that as an excuse not to find him today.

Even if I find out what's up, I don't have to do anything. Just pass the intel along to Olympias.

Yeah. Like that's going to happen.

Having run to the end of excuses, Valentine opened her inner eyes, and moved her soul stealthily away from her body.

As she left herself behind, Valentine whispered, "Here, Eddie, Eddie, Eddie."

He said, "Meet me at midday," but Char didn't really know what she was doing here. "Here" being a relative term for a place that existed both in her mind and outside her consciousness. Here was here because she, an immortal being, believed in it.

She wondered if her "here" would match Geoff Sterling's "here," and they would meet at midday.

"I don't know why I'm doing this," she complained.

"Because I asked you to."

She heard his voice, but turning around, she saw only gray emptiness. She instinctively knew the sun was at the center of the sky, but she hadn't gotten around to giving any distinct shape to their proposed meeting place.

"You didn't precisely ask," she told the disembodied voice of Geoff Sterling.

"I've seen your boyfriend," he answered. "Don't tell me you expect chivalry and gallant behavior from a man?"

"You're not a man," she pointed out. "And what I expect from a man is none of your business."

"Why not?" Sterling asked, suddenly popping into being in front of her.

Char took a step back, and suddenly felt sand warm under the soles of her bare feet. She looked down. Black sand. A warm, salt-scented breeze brushed her cheeks and ruffled her hair. She looked at Sterling.

"Hawaii," he explained. "There's black volcanic sand beaches in Hawaii. Black's our color, so I thought—"

"We're in Las Vegas," she reminded him.

He waved an arm. "We're anywhere we want to be in here."

Yeah. He was right about that. "I'm not here for romantic walks on beaches," she said, and immediately regretted her choice of words from the amused interest that suddenly flooded her senses. When she looked at him, he was grinning. "Oh, get over yourself, you ain't that pretty."

"Neither are you," he responded. "But I like you just fine the way you are."

"I am so pretty. Jebel thinks so," she added. This con-

versation was completely ridiculous, and totally off the point of what they should be discussing.

"Mortal opinions don't count."

She bristled at this. "That is so arrogant. And wrong."

Sterling looked away from her sharp regard, then shrugged, and looked at her again. "Yeah. Point taken. Jimmy wouldn't approve. Neither would Val. But I don't see what you see in your mortal."

She wasn't sure where Sterling wanted to go with this, but she wasn't going with him. Char concentrated, and turned the setting into them sitting at a table on a terrace overlooking the fountains at the Bellagio. She'd been tempted to plop them down in the stacks of a library, but why give him a chance to tease her about being all staid and proper? No reason not to talk business and enjoy a nice view.

"Las Vegas," she said. "Where we're supposed to be looking for the Scrolls of Silk."

"You take direction well, don't you?" Sterling observed. "Why are you listening to Val, anyway?"

"You are," she countered.

"Yeah, but I live with her."

Char took a sip from a tall glass of iced tea that appeared by her hand. In the distance she could see the outline of the Silk Road, its gilded and blue-tiled domes and towers glinting in the noonday sun. It looked gaudy as hell, as any temple to excess on the Strip should. It looked normal—but was she seeing it as it really was, or with her imagination?

"Imagination," Sterling said.

She looked at him. "Why couldn't we get there last night?" she asked Sterling. "What happened?"

"Think we can get there now?" he countered.

"I asked first. And I don't like trying to think about it, either," she added, feeling a certain amount of sympathy for both of them. After Valentine disappeared into the crowd last night, Char and Sterling started for the hotel at the other end of town. They'd decided to run, dodging through traffic, barely visible blurs on the edge of vision. It had been fun. But they were hit with something within a block or two of the Silk Road. Something that stopped them dead, left them confused, lost. Char barely made it back to her hotel before dawn. And she'd had a blazing headache. "It was weird."

"That is one term for magic," Sterling answered.

"You think they have a protective spell around the grounds? Is that what that pulse of energy was?"

"Felt like it to me."

"But if somebody at the Silk Road is spreading rumors about data hidden inside, doesn't that mean they want to lure magic users in?"

"If someone at the Silk Road is the one spreading the rumors. Have you actually traced the rumors there?"

"No," she had to admit.

Sterling ran a hand over his face. He glared at the hotel in their imaginations' distance. "Maybe—maybe it was a security measure."

"To keep vampires from gambling?" she suggested.

"We have a certain innate—luck—I suppose. We could use our psychic skills to cheat the casino. Of course, vampires run the casino and—"

"Maybe the place is warded to keep Nighthawks out."

"Now, there's a thought." She considered for a moment, sipped tea, then asked, "Think it's because of the Scrolls of Silk?"

"Probably. They're anti-Enforcer propaganda."

Char would have dropped her tea glass if it hadn't been imaginary to begin with. "You said you didn't know what the scrolls were."

He gave her a slowly growing smile. And his eyes glittered with amusement. "You always believe what you're told, don't you? Beside, I merely implied ignorance with my silence."

"Your friend said we'd go blind if we read them. I didn't believe that." Not really. But she kept it in the back of her mind. With magic you could never be too careful. A lot of people forgot that—and bad things happened to them.

"My friend should never be taken too literally. She has a very odd sense of humor. From what little I've heard, it's safer not to know about the scrolls. Safer not to tell a really old vampire you know about them. Val's really old."

"Why is it safer?"

" 'Cause people who read the scrolls get—uppity. Nighthawks made quick snacks of uppity strigoi even before they were called Enforcers and worked for the

Council. Nighthawks aren't even supposed to know what the scrolls say."

"Why?"

His smile grew even wider. "I think it's because what's written in the scrolls is true."

Her frustration was building. She got up and moved around the table toward Sterling. He stood to meet her. They met in the middle of the terrace, near a marble staircase that ran down to a deep aquamarine pool.

Toe to toe, she looked up at the much taller vampire and demanded, "What's in the scrolls? How do you know about them?"

He put his hands on her shoulders. Big hands. They were Nighthawks, with equal skills, strengths, and weaknesses. She wasn't used to that.

"Maybe you've been alone too much," he said.

"Answer my questions, Sterling."

"You were Jimmy's. Didn't he ever talk to you?"

Char refused to be wounded by the question. She barely noticed when his hands slid down her arms and he twined his fingers with hers. "Of course Jimmy talked to me. We talked all the time."

"About vampire things? The perks and hazards of eternal life? The responsibilities our kind owed mortals?"

She nodded. "Yes. About those sorts of things. He prepared me."

"Did he tell you you were Nighthawk?"

"No."

"Then he didn't prepare you. Or me. The change came as a complete surprise."

"It's supposed to. So that the ritual has more meaning."

"Bullshit. Vampires keep too many secrets."

"And this has to do with the scrolls, how?"

"Sorry. It's easy to get distracted when you finally have an equal to talk to."

She understood this. She appreciated it. "The sun's moving across the sky. Talk to me now, so we can do something when we wake up. Something's building, something that needs to be stopped. Can't you feel it?"

"Yes." He growled and, for a moment, showed hunting fangs. "And I hate it. I don't want to be involved. I really did come to town on business. And vacation. And because Val needs to get out more."

"And you were called here by fate. That happens to Nighthawks. No coincidences. Magic made us. Magic uses us. And you hate it."

He shrugged. "At least I met you. That makes up for some of the inconvenience."

She would have stepped back, but his grip on her hands tightened. She chose not to struggle. "And you still haven't told me anything useful. What did Jimmy tell you about the scrolls?" Why did he tell you and not me? She found her own pouting annoying, and hoped Sterling didn't notice it.

"I was a depressed, suicidal Goth kid when Jimmy approached me. I could feel everyone's pain, and wrote about it in very bad poetry. Thought the world and *everything in it was evil and doomed. Then I met a real vampire who told me to cheer up." He shook his head. "Jimmy's a teacher, a healer."*

Char's breath caught, and her heart ached with missing her first lover. "I know."

"He teaches that vampires, vampires like us, are meant to protect, to be superheroes. You were obviously ready to believe in his view of the underneath."

She nodded.

"I took a lot more convincing. I'm still not convinced, by the way. He told me about Nighthawks—not that I was going to be one—but about them. The Enforcer of Seattle wasn't exactly a prime specimen of the breed."

"I remember."

That Enforcer, and every vampire in Seattle, had eventually been executed or exiled for involvement in magic that used child abuse in dark rituals even most vampires found unforgivable. Istvan the dhamphir came in and wiped out a city's vampire population to put a stop to it. Char had the bad feeling that something similar was going to happen here. She had no evidence, but she trusted her instincts. And she hated being used by fate nearly as much as Geoff Sterling did.

"So, among the things Jimmy did to teach me the Bluecorn Way was he told me about this ancient document."

"The Scrolls of Silk."

"Said to be written in strigoi blood on scrolls—"

"Of silk."

"In the vampire city. Blah, blah, blah, very mysteri-

ous, protected by spells, so secret that the Nighthawks hunted down anyone who read it and wiped the memory from their minds. Or ate their hearts, which is a much more efficient way of making sure forbidden information doesn't get passed around."

"How did Jimmy know about the scrolls? He's not a Nighthawk."

"Yes he is. Just not a changed one."

"Of course. Still, how did he—?"

"He's a very old vampire. From the Bronze Age, at least. I think he started out as a tin trader from Cornwall and met the vampire who made him in one of the Greek city-states. And that's only my guess from things he said and things I've heard. I don't really know. What he told me about the Scrolls of Silk is that they claim that Nighthawks aren't really vampires."

Char laughed. "Excuse me? That's it?"

"It's a revolutionary idea."

"That's the stupidest—"

"But we're not really vampires, are we?" he questioned.

She found his enthusiasm daunting. "We start out as vampires."

"But we change. Grow into something different. We aren't vampires anymore. We hunt vampires. Consume them the way they consume mortals. What creature eats its own kind?"

"Rats and humans," she countered. "And—us."

He shook his head. "No. Nighthawks aren't vampires. So," he concluded.

"I don't think this conclusion is what Jimmy had in mind when he told you about the scrolls."

"No, it isn't. But I've always thought for myself. Only I hadn't thought about the scrolls in years, forgot about them until Val mentioned them last night. Maybe Jimmy wanted me to forget when the lesson didn't take."

"You sound awfully pleased to have remembered."

"It's a freeing concept."

"It's a stupid one. There's no proof."

There was no stopping his enthusiasm. "Why do we live under the same restrictions that limit the strigoi? The Laws don't apply to us."

That was when he pulled her close and kissed her.

Chapter 12

THE THING YOU always had to remember about Eddie
was that he was sneaky. Devious. Deceitful. He could
have played Gollum in the movie if the part hadn't already been taken. And he was a born con artist. His
biggest con was promising immortality to those who
couldn't have it. It was just plain cruel. And he wasn't
exactly stupid. Vain. Oh, yes, very vain. He could be
cowed, and threatened and coerced, but when you did
that to him, he was likely to turn on you in a secret,
slithering, poisonous way.

And I used to sleep with this guy?

Concentrate, Valentine chastised herself. The clock is
ticking here.

The trick was to approach him through his strengths
rather than his weaknesses. Let him remember his tri-

umphs and he wouldn't notice anyone there eavesdropping on his mental masturbation.

He felt her settling on him, into him, as nothing more than a passing dream of a woman he'd bedded long ago. The dream sent a shiver through him, but Valentine made sure the reaction merely reminded him of the damp cold of a bedchamber in a thick-walled castle. His castle, where he was the lord of all.

Those were the days, weren't they, Edward?

So they were. He nestled his head against her ample bosom.

These days are better.

Bitches rule the world.

But you outsmart them. You outsmart them all. Time and time again.

Time. That's what they always want.

Give me immortality or give me death, right?

Ha. Ha. Very funny.

You're the funny one. Always having the last laugh.

Can't give everyone what they want.

But you make them think you can. Like in Moscow. With the boy who bled.

Good scam. Too bad the boy had no gift.

History would have turned out differently.

I still miss Gregori. What a gift the monk had. That was the last time I used a companion as a front. Hurt too much when he was assassinated.

There, there. Valentine sent warmth and comfort to a psyche that still grieved for long-ago loss.

Better him than me, Eddie thought.

You don't need anyone's help, she coaxed, gentle and admiring, keeping disgust hidden. *You work wonders on your own. Like the last time you pulled a con. The most recent. Here in town. With—*

The skinny old coot.

Harsh laughter rippled through Eddie's mind, rippled over her like a heavy, wet blanket. One that smelled of swamp water.

Light addiction's a minor neurosis compared to his problems, Eddie's thoughts rolled on. *He was too easy.*

Maybe you made it look easy.

Eddie preened. *Maybe I did. He was so impressed when I just slipped past his guards one night. Sat on the end of his bed and promised that I could help him live forever. Did a few hypnotism tricks. Pulled on shadows, put on the masks.*

Impressed him.

Yeah. He had all the money in the world. I wanted it. We made a deal. His blood tasted like dust. He had enough gift to be a slave. He was—sickly when I found him. Press and his board of directors never knew how feeble he was. I started out to scam him, but turned out I did prolong his life. But he was crazy, really crazy. Tried to tame him, but the guards he kept around him suspected. They were all members of some kind of rigid Christian sect. Decided I was a devil.

Fools.

Lots of fools. More of them than me. Mortals always have us outnumbered. Better part of valor was to back off, let them take my meal ticket out of town. It lasted a few good years, though. He owned a lot of property in town. I made sure some of it was transferred to my name before they took him.

Good investment, real estate.

Land, and peasants to work it, that's true wealth.

Even without the peasants, property comes in handy. Helps to have a few places to hide.

Yeah. Things get hidden. I ain't going to take the blame.

She sensed his resentment, resistance, and fear. To go after the root of these things would bring up walls. She continued coaxing out clues instead. You still have this land?

Some.

Smart to hang on to property. They're always looking for land for new casinos.

Tell me about it. I've got an old warehouse near the airport. Going to sit on it awhile longer. It's worth millions to the resort developers already. I've got time. Property values in this town are always going up, up, up.

That's nice, sweetheart. Valentine began to drift away from Eddie's mind. She now had all she needed, and felt covered in mental muck from the time spent with her old lover. Go to deep, dark sleep now, she instructed him.

And whatever you do, don't dream of me.

It was not the scent of coffee that woke her. Char woke because that was what vampires did at sunset. But there was comfort in the scent of coffee, in knowing that there was someone from the daylight world that cared enough to have the warm drink waiting for her. A gift. A gesture of affection. Jebel Haven didn't have a warm, fragrant cup waiting for her every night; he wasn't even always there when she first came back to life. But waking now, knowing he was with her, that he cared—

Left her feeling a traitor. Dirty. Unfaithful.

It had only been a kiss. She hadn't instigated it. It had been without substance.

And it left her so aroused she woke blind with the need. Beyond the scent of coffee, overwhelming that dark richness, there was blood. There was flesh. There was need in him that ran near the surface as blue veins beneath fragile flesh.

"Jebel," she said, and reached for him.

Arms came around her, pulling her up, pulling her close. A mouth came down on Char's. She tasted coffee on his tongue. She drank him in, demanding. He was the first to moan with desire. The sound was muffled against her mouth, but roared through her.

She strained against his hands when they moved over her.

"Damn, woman!" he muttered, then sucked hard on one nipple, then the other.

One of the things she loved about Jebel was that he didn't ask questions in the bedroom. Didn't need to be seduced. He was always willing, always ready. And so very able. He gave her everything a man could.

Everything a mortal man could.

She forced the thought away. Forced herself not to

think at all. At least, as much as she could. She was so used to the ache in her mating fangs it had become a part of her arousal. Most of the time the need to taste him was something she could ignore. This wasn't most of the time.

"Damn, St—"

Jebel's head came up from her breast. "Wha—?"

"Damn, good," she said, and pushed his head back into the softness of her breast. "More!"

His lips closed on her hard nipple once more. She gasped with pleasure. And ran her fingers through thick, dark hair. Salt and pepper hair, she noticed. He wasn't getting any younger, and he led a hard life. His body was hard-muscled, his wits sharp—but he was mortal.

She could fix that.

She needed the taste of him on her tongue, salt copper sliding down her throat. A drop of him to quench her own thirst. Just a drop.

She was a creature of claws and fangs. He knew what he was getting with her. She was a wild thing. Dangerous to bed. He liked the danger, loved the razor's edge, knew he'd have to pay for the thrill.

And he was hers. Oh, yes. Hers.

Char ran her hands over the taut muscles of Jebel's back, caressed his buttocks and thighs. She kissed his shoulder and throat, scraped throbbing fangs against warm flesh. She breathed in the scents of sweat and lust—and the perfume of mortal decay. The subtle, constant, born in blood and muscle and bone smell of death was always mixed in with the vitality of life. There was no hint of fear in his emotions, only the fire of lust. He knew what she was, wanted her. Trusted her.

Not to turn on him. Not to take without asking.

Does he think I'm weak? a stray thought threaded through her desire.

Strong, a thought came back to her in Jebel's deep, rough voice. *Strong and beautiful.*

She wasn't used to his touching her like that, caressing her thoughts as well as her body. He was growing stronger, and reveling in that strength was aphrodisiacal for Char.

She came even before he entered her. When he did, her body arched in a spasm of pleasure, and she felt him respond through a sudden psychic link that was nearly as strong as a companion bond.

Love, he thought at her. Then he was lost to words, lost in visceral, male sensation.

She held him tight, vampire tight, leaving bruises, drawing a groan, and a dark, deep laugh. He pumped into her hard and fast then, a wild man answering the needs of a wild woman.

She needed this. Damn, how she needed this. She needed Jebel Haven.

Needed him so much that she didn't realize what she was doing until her mouth closed over his shoulder. She tasted the salt of sweat, felt the resistance of flesh, the erotic pop as the tips of mating fangs broke through the fragile barrier of skin. Then there was sex blood on her tongue, full of the rich, musky taste of hormones and heat.

Jebel howled, but not with pain. As she took a drop or two of rich red blood, Jebel stiffened against her, his orgasm filling her body and stabbing deep into her mind. Satisfaction settled on her like a heavy blanket, the same way Jebel covered her when he collapsed on her in a heavy, satiated heap.

She was greedy, wanting more blood, more sex. She was almost as hungry for it as a new-made vampire. How lovely it would be to lose herself in the craving, satisfaction, craving cycle that required no thought, no responsibility, no action outside of take, take, take.

She could do it, she knew. All she needed was to put out the DO NOT DISTURB sign on the door, then pin Jebel on the bed and have him the way a vampire was permitted to use any mortal with strong psychic gifts. Bleed him, fuck him, fuck him and bleed him. She wouldn't even have to make him a companion, though she'd have to be careful not to bleed him dry if she didn't give him her blood to replace the energy she drained from him.

It was only a selfish impulse, of course. She was a grown-up vampire, and didn't behave like that. Then again—if she changed the scenario, made it into a give and take—Jebel would be a vampire within a week.

What a glorious week it would be.

Then she'd never see him again, and that would be awful. Well, never see him was possibly an exaggeration, but they could never be together again as lovers, and that was awful.

And Geoff Sterling really had her rattled if she was

considering a scenario where all she had to do was exactly what she wanted for the amount of time it would take to get Sterling out of her head, and out of town as well.

The things he'd said, the things Sterling had done—kissing another vampire, for Goddess's sake! Maybe the Scrolls of Silk did make you go blind. Crazy, for sure. Geoff Sterling was crazy.

Worse, he was the snake holding out the apple. How did snakes hold out apples? With their fangs, she supposed. And Geoff Sterling had certainly extended his fangs when he kissed her. She'd felt them when their tongues twined and—

She hadn't remembered that she'd kissed Sterling back until this moment, and the memory sent a shiver she told herself was disgust through her. Had to be disgust, because she was too sated from making love with Jebel for it to be anything more intimate.

She sighed.

"What's the matter?" Jebel asked. His head was resting on her breasts, and the way his breath brushed across a nipple stirred warmth inside her once more.

"I want you again," she told him. This was the truth, even if it wasn't the truth that bothered her.

"But we have things to do," Jebel finished for her. With that, of course, he rolled off her and sat up, swinging his legs over the side of the bed. Jebel wasn't much for cuddling. "There's coffee."

"I know." She propped herself up on her elbows, and took a moment to appreciatively look at the length of his back and the width of his shoulders. "Smelled it when I woke up. Perfect aphrodisiac. Of course, it gets cold while we're fooling around."

"We weren't fooling, and it's in an insulated carafe."

"You never used to use words like *carafe*."

He grunted, then reached for the carafe on the bedside table, only to stop the motion and rub his shoulder. He turned his head to look at her. "You never used to be a biter."

She laughed. "Uh, Jebel—"

"Thought you were going to eat me alive for a second, sweetheart. That wasn't Little Mary Sunshine sex we were having."

Char fluttered her eyelashes at him in mock innocence. "You know very well I am not a man-eater, Mr. Haven. Not that type of girl, at all."

He continued rubbing his shoulder, though she knew very well the bite mark had already healed. "Uh-huh. Have I just lost my virginity?"

At least he didn't seem upset at her having bit him. "You were never a virgin."

He chuckled, and nodded, and put his hand over her breast. "Does this mean we're engaged?"

Char sat up, pushed pillows behind her back, took a cup of steaming coffee from Jebel with her right hand, and wiggled the fingers of her left. "I haven't seen a ring yet. And I haven't—" She saw the sudden look of amusement in his eyes, and found herself flustered. "I know this has never happened before. It was only a little. Harmless, really."

"Major rush, sweetheart. It's not going to turn me, is it?"

Of course he knew better than that. He was only teasing, but Char still felt compelled to explain, "You have to drink my blood for that. Mutual transfusions. I should have asked before I bit, but—"

"Heat of the moment." He leaned forward and kissed her forehead.

"Heat of passion," she answered. "I'm—hungry."

"Should have ordered a steak along with the coffee."

"Hungry for you," she asserted. Firmly. Maybe too firmly, because a certain speculative interest entered his gaze. "And I had really dirty dreams last day," she added.

"So, you spent the day fooling around while I was out working. Sweet life you have, McCairn."

She'd been working, but she didn't want to tell Jebel about it. Not because of Geoff Sterling, but because of the Scrolls of Silk. It seemed to her that the less anyone knew about these things, the better. So instead of bringing up her own activities, she asked, "What were you up to today?"

"Looking at the Scrolls of Silk among other things," he answered, casual as could be.

She would have jumped out of her skin, if it was possible while conscious. She did jump off the bed. Standing on the opposite side of the room from Jebel, she demanded, "What?"

He rose and turned to look at her, naked, tattooed, and

quite calm. "I was also looking for the missing Enforcer of the City. We have a lot to talk about, Charlotte." He watched her steadily, but with certain wariness beneath the calm. "But I suspect you know that."

Chapter 13

BEN WASN'T QUITE sure where he went to sleep, but he was certain this was not the place where he should be waking up. He vaguely remembered the scent and feel of leather. The coolness beneath him now felt like concrete. The smoothness that completely covered him was the texture of satin. It was an odd, disturbing combination. He resisted the impulse to move, to throw off the cloth that covered him. When he opened his eyes, he discovered the covering was striped in pink and orange. His sensitive night vision made him aware that the room beyond was brightly lit. He stayed quiet for now because he knew he was not alone. He was aware of mortal breath, a heartbeat, and the flow of warm blood. He could hear movement as well, and a low, almost subvocal muttering.

Ben felt like he'd been drugged. His head ached, his

memory was fuzzy, and he felt weak. How the hell did you drug a vampire? Who had done it, and why? Anger flared through him at the thought anyone would dare touch him. He snarled silently, and felt the prick of hunting fangs pressing on upper and lower lips before his jaw lengthened into a sharp muzzle to accommodate the growth of razor-sharp teeth.

It was hard to think through the weakness, harder to think through the transforming anger, but Ben managed to catch hold of his impulses. He stayed still. He brought his body back into mortal form. He took a few deep breaths, and made himself think. There was a current of energy in the air, surrounding him. He recognized where the weakness came from now. Who'd put a spell on him?

Martina. Her face drifted through his consciousness, all smug and bright-eyed with fanatical self-assurance. Had she done something to him? He hated her, but the truth was, she was barely aware of his existence. She didn't believe anyone but the Enforcers could pose a threat to her.

Who then?

What had he done last night? When he tried to remember, a fog rose up to blanket his thoughts. Aware now that this was a spell, Ben bent his will against it. He breathed the fog in like cigarette smoke and forced it to dissipate within him. He was a creature made out of magic, after all. Now. What had actually happened?

He'd given a spell book to Reese. Why hadn't he thought of that first? Because Reese had lulled him into a false sense of security. Or his own hormones had done that for Reese. They'd left the bar, gone back to Morgan Reese's dressing room. They'd talked. He'd talked more than Reese. Told him too much? Reese had been very pleased with the gift of the spell book. Far more than Ben had been. It was meant only as a gift, to earn Reese's trust, to please him, to impress him. Why would Reese use it against him?

Maybe he hadn't. Maybe Reese had tried out a spell, and it had gone wrong. The result was that Ben woke up confused and feeling like shit. Ben finally noticed that he wasn't restrained in any physical way. Reese had moved him, thrown a piece of cloth over him. That probably had a logical explanation. Maybe someone came knocking on the dressing room door during the day, and Reese had to quickly stash the body of a sleeping vampire before he answered the knock.

Logical. Reasonable. Sensible. Ben didn't quite believe it, and decided it was time to stop speculating and find out what was going on for himself.

The satin clung to him as he sat up, so he had the satisfaction of ripping the cloth apart with slightly extended claws.

Reese's back was to Ben. The sound of tearing fabric brought the mortal whirling around to face Ben. As their gazes met, Ben became aware that he was looking at Reese through the bars of a cage.

Ben laughed. It hid his disappointment in the man he was going to make his companion. It hid his anger. "So much for playing nice," he said.

He reached for the bars. Reese's smile was a warning, but Ben's fingers closed on the burning cold metal before he could draw them back. His howl of pain mingled with Reese's laughter.

Ben pulled his hands back and looked at the burn marks on his palms. "Maybe you should have mentioned that," he said from between gritted teeth.

Reese wiped a tear of amusement from the corner of his eye. "And missed your reaction? Wish you'd screamed longer," he added. "Pain and suffering come in handy."

"Really? For what?"

"Magic. Building magical energy."

"Where'd you hear that?"

Reese patted the spine of the notebook he held cradled in his arms. "In here. In the book you gave me."

Ben glared at Reese, and the notebook, and damned himself for a complete fool. He might not think much of magic, but it was real. Reese had inborn power, and Ben had given the mortal the keys to the treasure chest of the dark arts.

Reese came closer, but not so close that Ben could lunge at him through the bars. "Amazing how things respond to magic," he said, looking at the cage. "It's a flimsy thing, built to be collapsible, but with only a few words and a bit of concentration, I've made it a cage for a vampire." He laughed again, the sound low and full of genuine amazement. "A real vampire. When you admitted to it last night, I thought you were crazy. Even feeling the power—" He gestured with one hand across the room where the red jewel and gold cup sat on the polished black marble coffee table. He continued to clutch the book tightly to his chest. "Look at that thing."

Ben glanced at his other gifts to Reese. The gold cup looked somehow brighter, richer than the shining object he remembered. The jewel—it wasn't just gleaming with the fire of a huge, multifaceted ruby anymore. It wasn't reflecting light, but glowing with its own inner fire. And waves of heat shimmered the air around it.

"It looks bigger," Ben said.

"It reacts to magic. I've been doing a lot of magic while you were sleeping." He glanced toward the door, then toward the ceiling. "I'm going to have to make you scream again."

Ben laughed. "There is a lot of screaming in one of our futures."

Reese ignored the threat. "Dark magic requires pain."

"Yes," Ben agreed with Reese. "Pain, fear, and death will make you into a vampire. Believe me, I will give you a great deal of pain and fear before I let you use the spell that will bring you rebirth."

Reese focused his attention back on Ben. "You promised me immortality last night."

"I still intend to give it to you." Ben gestured toward the cage bars, but carefully didn't touch them. His palms were healing, but they still hurt. He wasn't going to injure himself if he could talk his way out instead. "I admire your initiative—your experimentation—but you really don't want me pissed with you."

Reese gave him a look that was downright coy.

"You're not pissed at me now?" Before Ben could answer, Reese turned toward the door. "Well," he said mildly. "You will be in a moment."

Ben felt her coming before she reached the door. Frantic, afraid for him, protective. Emotions guaranteed to make her careless as she rushed to her lover's aid. Ben didn't know what Reese intended to do to his companion, but Ben wasn't going to let it happen.

He grabbed the bars, twisting the freezing metal with all his strength as the door opened. At the same time he shouted through the rising pain. "Get out of here, Clare!"

He didn't know if she heard him, or responded to the order. The world went bright, searing red. Ben dropped hard onto his knees, and the world went black. It lasted only a moment. He came back to consciousness in time to catch himself before slumping completely onto the concrete slab. Ben hissed as his burned palms hit the rough flooring, but he pushed himself up, surging to his feet with supernatural speed.

Reese had the notebook open. He was speaking swiftly, softly. Ben couldn't make out the words, but the sounds hurt his ears. The temperature in the room rose as Reese spoke the incantation. Clare's back was pressed against the closed door. Her eyes were on Ben, wide with fear. Sweat covered her as she strained to move.

Ben hated seeing her like that. Hated knowing he was the cause of her distress. "Stop it," he called to Reese. "Leave her alone or I'll rip your fucking heart out."

Reese did shut up, but Ben knew it had nothing to do with the threat. It was because Reese had completed the spell.

The magician closed the notebook, but still held it close as he turned back to Ben. "Rip my heart out? What an interesting thing to say. Your girlfriend can speak," he added. "But she can't move. She can't help you, but at least you can have a conversation while I get ready."

"Ready for what?" Ben demanded. He had the feeling Reese planned to put on a magic show, but not one that had anything to do with the stage tricks that made him famous.

Once Reese was gone out through a different door, Ben asked Clare, "You okay?"

Her eyes were wild. "No."

He tried to send reassurance through their psychic link, but doubted anything but Reese's psychic powers worked inside this room.

"I should have come sooner. I should have helped you sooner."

Clare's eyes and voice held so much guilt and self-loathing, it turned Ben's stomach. Right now he hated himself, hated the way he'd bound her to him. He'd once been bound to Alice. That was the way of the vampire life. That didn't always make it right. Not when it put Clare in danger.

"I should be the one protecting you," he told her. "I got myself into this. You warned me about Reese. I should have listened."

"It's your right," she defended Ben to himself.

"That's crap," he told her. "And we both know it."

A flash of anger flared in her eyes, like lightning in a distant desert storm. "It's the Law," she said. "We both know it."

"And you want to change the Laws."

Fear replaced the anger. New fear. Not for him, but of him. "You—know?"

Ben waved a hand in front of the bars of his cage. "It's pretty obvious I don't know anything. Never mind, sweetheart." He glanced to the spot in the ceiling where a small camera watched the room. "What did he do to your security system?"

"Don't know, exactly. But the monitor in Control shows that you're still sleeping. I wasn't in Control when I felt you wake up. Didn't suspect anything until I got back and checked the screen. Then you screamed. I ran. Was too upset to tell anyone to come with me. Sorry."

Ben shrugged. "We'll work it out."

As he spoke, Morgan Reese returned. This time he was carrying what looked like a large pair of quilted silver oven mitts. He put them down on a chair, then took everything but the glowing red gem off the marble-topped coffee table. "This will have to do," Reese said. He went over to Clare and took her by the shoulders. He smiled at her. "I need a volunteer. Come along," he urged and pulled her toward the table. "I need you to lie down."

"You've read the Scrolls of Silk?"

Haven didn't think Char noticed her voice rise to a

near shriek as she shouted. He waved a hand to shush her. "I said I saw them. From a distance. Through a surveillance camera." This gave too much away, and he cursed himself for it. "There's some things you need to know," he went on. "If you don't ask questions."

She gave him a stern look. The sort of look that reminded him that she was a cop. A cop who could rip any information she wanted out of his mind if she chose to. Fortunately, mindrape was not something Char would ever immediately consider. She asked, "Questions about how you get your information?"

"I have sources," he said. "I need to protect them. Like a journalist."

"Protect them from me?" Her hands were on her naked hips, and there was, literally, fire in her eyes. At least they were glowing in an angry vampire way.

"Yes," he answered. Never back down from an angry vampire was Haven's policy. He'd survived so far. "Look at you, going Enforcer on me when I'm trying to help you."

"I am an Enforcer. I am a Nighthawk."

For some reason she blushed when she said it, and her gaze slid away from his in a guilty kind of way. What was up with that?

"You worried about what's in the scrolls?" he asked. "Think I won't love you if you aren't really a vampire?"

"I am a vampire!" Char actually stamped her foot when she said it. "Whatever you've heard is a lie."

Haven held his hands up in front of him. "Hold on,

Char. Darlin', I do *not* know what the scrolls say. I haven't read them. I'm guessing about them. And the guess seems to have hit a nerve. Hit a nerve with people who have fangs and it can get ugly."

This made Char smile a little. "You're making a very educated guess." Her eyes were no longer glowing, but there was sharp suspicion in them. "How?"

"I know why I'm really in Vegas," he said. He sat down on the bed and patted a spot on the rumpled bedding for her to join him. "Neither of us came only for the wedding, and we both know the other knows it. Why are *you* really in Vegas?"

"The Silk Road," she admitted, sitting down beside him. "All I wanted was to have a look inside the Silk Road. It's supposed to be full of wonderful things."

He scratched his chin. "I was in the museum today," he told her. "I don't know how you vampire cops let it happen, but the place is full of real stuff. Very scholarly. You'll love it. You should go." He put an arm around her shoulders, pulled her close. "But you have to take care of Martina first."

Her surprise went through him like a hot knife. Char jerked away. "Martina? Who the hell's Martina?"

"The vampire nest leader responsible for the Enforcer of Las Vegas's disappearance."

She was on her feet again. "How did you know he disappeared? At least, Valentine thinks he's disappeared—though I don't know who the hell Valentine really is, or why I feel compelled to listen to her."

The name *Valentine* had come up on the companions' conspiracy board, but Haven wasn't prepared to mention his rebellious activities to Char just yet. "Let's not make this too complicated," he told her. "Never mind this scroll shit. Words *can* kill you if you're allergic to magic, but fangs and claws and weapons can kill you faster."

"I don't think the scrolls have anything to do with spells. The scrolls contain negative propaganda about the Nighthawks. The information can be used to turn regular vampires against us. Those words can kill us even without containing magic."

Char was a great believer in words. "Actions speak louder than words, isn't that the saying?"

She nodded. "Yes. But—"

"Let's stick to immediate danger. What I've discovered in Las Vegas is a situation involving a nest of vampires who hate Enforcers. If they're going to—what?—post the scrolls online? That's probably only part of this Martina's plan. Who believes in old prophecies and that kind of crap these days? How many care? Modern vampires believe in science. Most people turned into vampires in the last fifty years think it's caused by a mutation that affects their reaction to energy fields."

"How do you know that?"

He ignored the question. "Some have never heard your creation myth. Some believe the origin stories about vampires in movies and comic books. Am I right?"

She nodded reluctantly. "You've been thinking too much, Jebel."

"Comes from hanging with you, babe. Now, if Martina feeds regular vampires scientific information, gives them DNA evidence that Nighthawks are different than they are, then the vampire population's going to get restless on your Nighthawk asses."

She frowned at his language, then said, "Well put, Jebel. You have such a way with words."

"I do," he agreed. He crossed his arms. "So, Enforcer McCairn, what do you think's going on when a nest of Nighthawk-hating vampires goes looking for the local Enforcer, and that Enforcer then disappears?"

She didn't have to think about this long. "I think the Enforcer is a dead-brained dickless asshole if he lets himself be taken by a few disgruntled vampires."

It was his turn to frown at her language. "Well put, Charlotte."

"We need to find this nest," she announced, "and the idiot Enforcer they're doing lab work on. We probably need to get dressed before we do that," she added.

Haven rose to his feet. "I've got an idea. Why don't you go back to Tucson, and let me track down this Martina and her disgruntled nest."

She looked amused, and pleased, at his concern. "You're trying to protect *me*?"

He nodded, quite solemnly, aware in that moment that he was afraid for her. "They're out to get Nighthawks," he reminded her. "You're a Nighthawk. Why offer them another target?"

She touched the spot on his shoulder she'd bitten earlier. "You're going to be a Nighthawk." She gave him a fierce grin. "Let's go get them together. But first we get dressed. And I have to call Valentine." After a disturbing hesitation, she added reluctantly, "And Sterling."

Chapter 14

"WHY DO I have to be here?" Eddie saw Martina wince at his whining. So he whined some more. "Why? I've got a life, you know."

"Don't you want to see how we've fixed up the place, wraith?" She gestured around them.

Eddie only vaguely remembered how the hangar building had looked in its prime. One end had an open space under an arched roof big enough to hold a couple of small private airplanes. A wall separated the hangar area from several rooms that had once been used as an office, and living quarters for the flight crews of the planes. Eddie knew Martina hadn't sent a pair of big boys from her nest to fetch him for the purpose of showing off the redecorating.

He'd been brought through the dark hangar to meet Martina in the old office area. The place had changed a

lot. The smell of the fresh white paint on the walls bothered his nose. There was disinfectant in the air as well,
and even a hint of lemon from the polish on the floors. The
new lighting fixtures might be bright by mortal standards,
but they did nothing for Eddie's needs. The place held lab
benches, where mortals worked with high-tech machines.
About the only things Eddie could identify were several
high-powered-looking microscopes. There was a lot of
glass around, beakers and test tubes and whatnot.

Martina already had a hand on his shoulder; now she
squeezed it. "This place was a trash heap, with rats and
homeless people inside before we started. You should
thank us, wraith."

"Maybe I should raise your rent," he muttered.

"In a few hours our slaves and companions turned
your wrecked property into the lab and holding facility
we require."

"You have clever slaves," he answered. He was not
impressed. What did he care about the education of
mortal monkey puppets?

"Very clever," Martina agreed. "This operation has
been in the planning stages for nearly a decade."

"A decade's not that long."

"In the growth of mortal scientific knowledge, the last
decade has been amazing. I've been following the de-
velopment in genetic research, and knew it held the key
to our finding proof about the abominations. It did take
some time to find the type of scientists we needed, people with training, skills, and of course, enough of the
Goddess's Gift to be put to our uses. As soon as we

heard about Ibis's plans to bring the city back to life in the modern age, we put my plan in motion. We made a bargain with him to exchange information for our services. We found and enslaved our research team. We acquired the necessary equipment—"

"Which you kept in a truck because you didn't have anywhere to stash it."

She ignored, or possibly didn't notice, Eddie's sarcasm. "We found you. We knew you had property."

Eddie wanted to snap at her that there were a lot of things she didn't know about him. But what was the point? All he really wanted was to find out why she'd brought him here, and then get out. It was bad enough he'd had dreams about Martina last day; he didn't want to face the fanatic in the flesh any longer than he had to. He glared at her now, waiting.

She was silent under his regard for a few moments, then she smiled, like a kid with a very special secret. "Do you want to see what we're doing to the abomination?"

"No," he said.

She ignored him, and drew him down a hall to a heavy door that was guarded by two of the biggest vampires Eddie had ever seen. Not only were this pair tall, broad, and heavily muscled, but they wore body armor, helmets, and held heavy guns. Now this show of strength impressed Eddie. He was a warrior, after all.

Martina urged him forward. Eddie balked, and pointed toward the door. "You're keeping Duke in there?"

"It's perfectly safe." Her smile was smug, even placid. "He's drugged. And restrained."

"He's an Enforcer!"

"That's that sort of attitude we're trying to save you people from." She shook her head. "You're terrified of him, aren't you?"

"And you're not?" Eddie pulled away from Martina's grip, but one of her guards stepped forward and leveled his weapon at Eddie's chest. Eddie was not normally afraid of guns, but something about the barrel of this thing looked ominous. He shot a look at Martina. "What kind of rounds does that thing fire?"

"Incendiary," she answered. She was smiling benignly again. "Very painful."

"Vampires can't kill vampires."

He'd always truly believed this was the one evil that strigoi could not commit on each other. But now, with the way this nest of insane fanatics acted, he was no longer so sure.

"*I* don't want to kill you, wraith."

Eddie didn't like the emphasis on *I*. "What do you want?"

"A sample of your blood." She gestured toward the door. "Let's go inside."

Jebel didn't tell me why he's in town.

Char recalled this while she sat on the bench she'd shared with Valentine the night before. Lights flared in pretty patterns overhead, and neon blinked and swirled at the entrances to casinos. Char had no problem ignoring the lights, or the pedestrian traffic all around her. Even the vampire junkies were no more than tiny blips on her awareness. She was in a broody mood, and Jebel Haven was easy to brood over.

While their conversation in the hotel was supposed to have been a two-way information exchange, she'd blurted out her interest in the hotel—which she supposed wasn't all that big of a secret—but Jebel hadn't really told her anything. Except about Martina, the scrolls, and the missing Enforcer, she amended. Okay, so he had told her a lot, but he hadn't told her *why*. He hadn't told her *how*. He hadn't named sources. It was important in their very secret world to keep it secret. She shouldn't let a mortal keep important information from her. She shouldn't let a mortal freely snoop around the edges of vampire life. Of course, she shouldn't have let him go so long without having tasted her blood, either. Their bond was real, and it was strong, but it was a human one, made up of trust, and love. It was too human. She acted too human. And that was no way for an Enforcer to protect her kind.

"I'm going to nail him," she vowed to the night. "Tonight. Going to drag him into an alley if I have to, cut a vein, and make him take a drink." If they could find a few minutes to spare from saving the local Enforcer from whatever trouble he'd gotten himself into. She ran her tongue over slightly extended mating fangs. "Going to be sweet."

Fortunately, the night around her was too busy, and far too noisy for anyone to overhear her talking to herself. This was the sort of place where people gave you space. People came here to enjoy themselves. To make fools of themselves. They got drunk and noisy and rowdy and made out with each other. No one paid attention to anyone else, or expected anyone to pay attention to them. It was permanent Mardi Gras. She could feel their joy, frantically desperate in many cases, but at least mortals knew how to have fun. There was a certain built-in gloominess to being a vampire. She liked humanity.

Maybe it would help if she didn't like humans so much. Maybe it would be better for her if she didn't believe, deep in her soul, that she was human, just diurnally challenged. Many vampires thought they gave up their humanity when they changed, which accounted for the lack of a sense of fun. Now she found out that some vampires didn't think Nighthawks were vampires. She felt like some evil conspiracy was trying to throw her out of her species, not once, but twice.

"And I won't have it," she murmured, firm and fierce.

She wondered where Geoff Sterling stood on the humanity issue. And why he liked the notion that Nighthawks were utterly different than the parents they came from. She also wished she wasn't sitting here waiting for Sterling and the enigmatic Valentine to put in an appearance.

"Stupid meeting place," she muttered as she took a look at the rapt faces of the tourist crowd fascinated by the light show around them. "Stupid people." Why did she feel so compelled to take care of them? Even the neon junkies wandering among the mortals got a certain amount of her sympathy.

Maybe she shouldn't have called Valentine and Sterling in. She and Jebel were certainly capable of handling a few rogue vampires. She was very aware of Jebel as he roamed restlessly up and down the five-block area. He was guarding the perimeter, guarding her from the neon junkies, she supposed. Or more likely, the alert monster hunter part of him was uneasy about the presence of so many vampires dispersed among the crowd of mortals.

"Probably a bit of both," Valentine said, suddenly standing next to the bench. "Who is he?" she asked as Char jumped to her feet. "He's cute."

"But mortal," Sterling added from behind her.

"He has a cute butt," Valentine said.

"She's been following your boyfriend for a few minutes," Sterling said when Char turned to face him. "I thought she was checking to see if he's dangerous to us." He grinned and shrugged. He was wearing sunglasses again. They were all dressed in black. "Guess she was just checking him out."

"Dark, dangerous, dirty. Qualities I like in a man."

Char did not like the other woman's casual tone. It made her claws want to come out. "He's mine."

"And she's mine," Jebel said, coming up to stand closely behind Sterling. "You understand that, don't you, fang boy?"

So, Jebel had noticed Sterling's interest in her. Char was pleased by this show of possessiveness on Jebel's part.

Sterling stood preternaturally still, his expression going flat. "Don't annoy me, mortal."

"I won't like you when you're annoyed?" Jebel spoke with confident amusement. He glanced at Valentine. Char noticed he took a moment to appreciate the other vampire's feminine attributes, then he looked at her, smiling. "These your friends, sweetheart?"

"I wouldn't call them friends," she replied. "But I think we're going to need their help," Char admitted as a sudden burst of anxiety overcame her. She looked around anxiously, then was compelled to meet Valentine's dark gaze. "Something's—"

"Stirring," the older vampire said. Valentine exhaled, then took a deep breath. "Something." Then she seemed to shake off any semblance of worry, and smiled at Jebel. "While we're waiting for disaster to strike, you can fill us in on what we need to know."

"What the hell do you think you're doing?" Ben demanded.

Reese ignored him, and continued unbuttoning Clare's shirt. He had her stretched out on the low table, paralyzed, but her face was turned toward Ben.

Ben reached out to shake the cage, despite the agony. Clare's eyes were on him, full of terror and pleading, but she was completely in Reese's control. "You'll die if you hurt her," Ben promised.

Reese was going to die, Ben decided. No way did Ben want to take a person with so much magical power into the strigoi world. Clare had warned him Reese was ambitious and no good. He'd known it, and was amused by the prospect of taming a tiger, just as he'd been tamed. But Ben knew he'd never been all that dangerous. He'd wanted simple power, money, dames, to build an empire, sure, but a business one.

"You want to rule the world, don't you?" he called to Reese.

At this question, Morgan Reese straightened up from looming over Clare and turned to face Ben. "I worshipped Satan as a teenager," he told Ben. "Took part in the black mass. We sacrificed chickens, dogs. We drank their blood. But the magic didn't work. It was stupid, humiliating. Turned me off to the idea of real magic. So I took up stage magic and was good at it. But real magic still drew me. Drew me here. To this place. Called me." Reese smiled in a way that Ben found sickening. "Now I realize that if I'd been the one performing the rituals back in my Satanist days, I'd have ruled the world long ago."

"Ruled the world?" Ben exploded. "Are you crazy? You think magic—Listen to me, you idiot. Charisma's the only kind of magic that works on most people. Ritual shit hardly works on anybody."

Reese ignored him and turned back toward Clare. He flipped through pages in the notebook, then picked up the oven mitts.

Fear twisted through Ben. "Don't do this," Ben pleaded. "It's not going to help you rule the world. It's not worth the effort. Magic doesn't work!"

"It works on you," Reese said without looking toward Ben.

"Yes, but—"

"It works on things. It binds the universe together."

"That's the Force, you idiot!"

"Same thing," Reese said.

He moved in front of the table, blocking Ben's view of Clare. He held his arms up and out to the sides and began to chant. The heavy gloves looked ludicrously out of place in a magical ritual. Ben grew dizzy as Reese continued to speak. He couldn't make out the words, but the sounds fell into his mind, almost glowed inside his head. The gathering power took his breath away. Energy swirled around the room, drawn toward Reese. Ben felt the rush of current like razor cuts scraping across his skin. Pain blinded him until the voice stopped, and the world and the magic were poised in the silence, waiting for what Reese would do next.

"No," Ben begged, knowing what must come now, even before it began.

Waves of heat shimmered up from the ruby. Fire glowed in its heart. Reese picked it up, very carefully. He moved quickly, smoke rising from the heat-resistant padding of the gloves. Ben caught a brief glimpse of Clare's face before Reese stood poised over her again. He saw her terror, and her tears, and the plea for help in her eyes.

"No," Ben said again. He shook the cage again, totally unaware of his own pain.

Clare had no voice to scream when the burning ruby

touched her flesh. But Ben knew the instant her pain started, and screamed for her. He was exquisitely aware of Clare's agony, and the reek of charring flesh and burning blood. He knew when the stone burrowed into her chest cavity and first touched her heart.

That was when Morgan Reese began chanting again.

Chapter 15

"WHY DO YOU need my blood? Why do we have to go in there?" Duke was in there. Eddie didn't want to go anywhere near a pissed-off Enforcer. Not even one who was tied down and drugged. Not even Duke.

Nobody listened to him. One of the guards opened the heavy door. The other one pushed him in behind Martina, then followed after and made sure the door was closed and locked again. Eddie checked quickly for exits. Of course, the door was the only way in or out. Damn.

For some reason he'd expected to see Duke stretched out on an operating table, hooked up to all kinds of monitoring equipment, and with a bunch of mortal scientists poking and prodding at him. There were mortals in the room; they were even wearing white lab coats. There was monitoring equipment, and a metal table, but it was empty. Duke was in the room, all right, off in one corner, naked and looking like hell. Eddie couldn't see anything high-tech about the way the Nighthawk was being restrained. There was a metal collar around Duke's neck. A heavy chain fastened the collar to the wall.

"The wall's reinforced, right?" Eddie asked nervously. "The chain's going to hold him?"

"Of course," Martina answered with blithe self-confidence. "Modern materials are wonderfully strong."

Eddie noticed the nervous glances the mortal slaves threw Duke's way as they went about their mistress's business. "You sure?"

Martina moved closer to Duke, taking Eddie with her. "Pitiful creature," she said happily.

The Enforcer's head came up slowly. His expression was full of pain, not exactly vacant, but not really aware, either. He snarled weakly, but without a hint of any sort of fang showing.

Eddie wanted to bolt, but since he was held fast by the stronger vampire, he indulged his curiosity instead. "What kind of drugs work on Nighthawks?"

"Potent ones," was the smug answer. "We're letting them wear off a bit now. There's an experiment to be performed that he needs to be awake for."

Eddie forgot about Duke's plight, and gulped. "You're not going to experiment on me, are you?"

"No." Martina smiled. "We aren't interested in monitoring your responses."

"You said you wanted my blood."

"My scientists want a blood sample from you." She took him over to a counter where a trio of mortals stood waiting. One of them held a large syringe.

Eddie experienced a type of fear he'd never known before at the sight of the sharp needle. "You're not going to stick me with that thing, are you?"

"You're a vampire, wraith," Martina reminded him. "You're used to fangs penetrating your skin."

"That's different. It is," he insisted at Martina's exasperated look. "Besides, a needle won't go through our skin." He took some hope from this.

Hope Martina immediately dashed. "This needle will."

"I don't want to," he declared. "It's not right. Not Lawful. Vampires only give blood when they're dating."

"This is for a good cause," Martina countered. "For science. We're gathering blood samples from as wide a range of vampires as we can. We're gathering data that will help our kind. Within a few years we hope to find cures for your light sensitivity, and the agoraphobia that plagues others of our kind. With scientific knowledge we can help ourselves."

Eddie was shocked to his core. "The Laws forbids experimentation. The Law—"

"That's what the Enforcers have taught us to believe. We've been lied to, kept in the dark ages. Enforcers must—"

"No!" Eddie held up a hand. "Don't start." He looked at the lab technician slave with the syringe. "I'd rather give a blood sample than listen to another rant."

Martina finally let him go, and the slave stepped forward. Eddie closed his eyes, and turned his head away. "Will it hurt?"

"Yes," the tech answered.

Eddie did not appreciate the honesty, but he stayed still rather than follow the urge to rip the slave's head off when the metal penetrated his skin.

After a few minutes, the tech said, "Done."

Eddie sighed with relief and opened his eyes. He looked at Martina, who stood there with her arms crossed, looking smugger than ever. "Can I go now?" he asked her.

"I'm sorry, wraith," she answered, though there was nothing but glee in her. "But letting you go would be a waste of resources." Fear clutched in Eddie's gut as she looked back at Duke. "We've taken a lot of blood out of him," she said. She looked back at Eddie. "He's getting hungry."

Vampires sated their need for renewed energy by consuming mortals. Nighthawks built up their strength by taking the energy from vampires. It was a food chain thing.

"No. You can't do this!" Eddie backed away from the mortals, but was grabbed from behind by a couple of vampires. He struggled, and pleaded with Martina. "Please, don't. You can't do this to me!"

"I have to, wraith," she answered. "We need to record the physiological changes the abominations exhibit when they feed. We need that data, and I'm certainly not going to throw one of my people to that monster."

"You said you weren't going to experiment on me."

"We aren't," Martina answered. "No one's interested in the meat's opinion of being eaten. Rouse the abomination," she ordered her slaves. "Bring him," she ordered her vampires.

Eddie realized he wasn't going to be the main course immediately when his captors began to drag him toward the door. They were going to stash him somewhere, weren't they? Lock him up until feeding time? Good. Good. Maybe there was a chance he could—

Then a hot wind out of hell blew through his brain. He dropped to the floor like a rock, and was vaguely aware of everyone else in the lab doing the same. He heard retching. Smelled vomit. A horrifying howl rose out of the corner where Duke was chained. Then the darkness came.

When the lights went out, Eddie prayed it was some kind of electrical problem. Panic rose instantly, worse than the fear of being eaten alive. Worse than the mental blow a moment before. His terror turned into a long, drawn-out scream. He hated and feared darkness like nothing else in the world.

Soon, he realized he wasn't the only one screaming. For some reason, not being in it alone helped bring him back from the edge. Opening his eyes helped him remember what he was. He could see well in the dark, better than most vampires. Even a windowless room wasn't truly dark, especially where there were mortals to give off the faint glow of living energy. He, more than the normal vampires in the lab, could see a little. He didn't have to be a vampire to hear the bellowing of the enraged Enforcer, the rattle and rip of chains issuing from Duke's corner. There was no mind behind the monster screams, no intelligence, but rage and hunger howled in the dark. This was not good.

And no one, not even Martina, was stupid enough not to recognize the danger. "Sedate him!" she shouted out of the dark. "Get him under control. Get that collar back on him!"

"Get the lights back on!" someone else shouted.

"Get the hell out of here," Eddie advised, and ran for the door.

With one glance back, Eddie saw that Duke wasn't the only strigoi that had gone into fang-and-muzzle hunter mode. His own jaw ached, hunting fangs trying to pop out, but he managed to get the urge under control. He had the feeling the ones who'd changed hadn't done so to protect themselves from the Hunter. There was some bad magic doing some genetic tinkering all on its own. He wondered how Martina would try to explain that, and sincerely hoped she'd get eaten in midexplanation.

He didn't look back again, but he heard the ominous snap and rattle as the chain separated from the wall. Duke was loose. A moment later someone screamed in agony. The smell of blood filled the air. Panicked mortals and vampires rushed behind him, bumping into each other. There was swearing and screaming, and Martina shouted for calm and obedience.

The lights came back on as Eddie reached the door. He still didn't look back. He yanked the door open.

There must have been a hell of a lot of soundproofing in place, because the guard in the hall looked surprised at the sight of Eddie. There was also blood coming out of the guard's ears, so maybe he'd had a really bad reaction to the energy surge.

Eddie didn't care. He was getting out of there right now. He only paused long enough to head-butt the guard and grab the huge gun from him as people poured out the door behind him.

Eddie figured that with a crazed Nighthawk and a few hunting vampires on the loose, having any kind of weapon might come in handy.

"That's all very interesting, mortal," Geoff said when Haven was finished. "Where did you get your information? How do we know you're telling the truth?"

"I don't answer to you," Haven said.

They didn't like each other. Valentine could tell. The pair were standing toe to toe in the center of the crowded sidewalk, hostile energy crackling between them. The two males were very much alike, both good-looking, one in a rough way, the other Hollywood smooth. Geoff was a bit taller, Haven a bit more muscular. Both were obviously dangerous, and thoroughly alpha. The pair occupied an invisible energy bubble, people instinctively staying out of their way no matter how crowded the busy tourist area was.

"His name isn't 'mortal,' " Char said after drawn-out silence became too tense for her to bear. She'd been pacing nervously while the two males faced off. She confronted Geoff now. "His name is Jebel Haven, and he's on our side."

"Is he?" Geoff wondered, voice soft as velvet.

Valentine was aware of the ebb and flow of energy crackling between the trio. There was a great deal of soap opera potential to the situation, and Val didn't like it at all. She thought part of it might have to do with the general weirdness of the atmosphere. She chose to call it the Fraught Factor. Part of it . . . Well, she and Geoff would have to have a talk about birds, bees, and silver daggers that slid into your heart for making naughty moves on your sister some other time.

"Right now," she said, "the night isn't getting any younger, oh my children, and friends of the family." She gave a long look at the scrumptious Mr. Haven. "Right now we need a plan, not a rumble between the Jets and the Sharks."

"We?" Haven asked.

"Jets and Sharks?" Geoff asked, glancing at her over the top of his sunglasses. "Rumble?"

"Drive-by, then," she amended, acceding to modern vernacular. "We still need a plan." Haven was frowning at her. "Yes, dear?"

"Who died and made you Fearless Leader?" he asked.

"A lot of people," she replied.

He smiled. "Thought so."

He was fearless himself. She found that very attractive.

Char put herself between Valentine and Haven. "Well, then," she demanded. "What do we do about Martina?"

"Hunt her down and kill her," Geoff suggested.

"Works for me," said Haven.

"There we are, then," Val said, with an offhand gesture. "Sounds like a plan."

"But . . ." Char looked totally baffled. Apparently the young Enforcer expected something more along the lines of a formal debate.

Valentine put a comforting hand on Char's shoulder. "I bet you report to someone, don't you?"

"Yes. Istvan."

Valentine smiled with delight. "Really? He's such a nice boy. Tell him Val says hello."

"Istvan the *dhamphir* . . . a nice . . ." Char trailed off helplessly, and looked back at Haven. "He's . . ."

"The meanest mother in the valley," Haven supplied. "Or so I've heard it said," he added when Valentine and Char gave him questioning looks.

"Val," Geoff broke in sharply. "Could we get back on topic?"

"Martina hangs out at the Silk Road," Haven said. "Her nest run the place."

"Which means that marching into the hotel to tear out her heart might meet with some resistance," Char said.

"Don't you want to take out her whole crew anyway?" Haven questioned. "And get your hands on the scrolls? What I saw were Xeroxed pages," he added. "No scrolls involved."

"I'd definitely like to have a look at them, whatever form they're in," Geoff said.

"Destroy them, you mean," Valentine corrected. "It's forbidden to read them."

Geoff balked at this. "Maybe for vampires. We're Nighthawks. I want to know what's been written about us."

"It's rude," Val replied. "Very unflattering."

"But is any of it true?" he wanted to know.

She wished he hadn't asked. "It's propaganda written to discredit the Nighthawks a long time ago. The scrolls were not written by Nighthawks, Geoffrey. How can anyone know what we are without being of our line?"

Haven spoke up. "Are we going to kill vamps tonight, or what?"

Valentine and the other Nighthawks stared at him. "We?" Geoff finally asked.

Haven produced a key card with his photo on it out of a coat pocket. "I can get you into any part of the hotel. I even know what this Martina looks like."

"Mortals aren't allowed to kill vampires," Char said.

He gave her a hard look. "We've had this discussion before." They glared at each other for a moment. He didn't back down, but he did shrug. "Fine. You kill the nest vamps. I'll take the slaves and companions."

Char visibly relaxed. "Deal."

"Wait a minute," Geoff complained. "You can't let this mort—"

"It's against the Laws for mortals to be involved," Val cut in smoothly, drawing their attention back to her. "You disapprove of the Laws, Geoffrey. I think the

Council's full of shit. You and I have no argument with
Mr. Haven lending a hand if Char agrees to it." Char
gave Geoff a smug look. Val went on. "Of course, if
we're going to rescue Duke and kill us some bad vampires, the hotel's probably not where we should be looking. For that, we need the airport."

"Why? They've left town?" Haven questioned.

She ignored his sarcasm. "We need to find where
Martina's holding Duke prisoner. We have to look for an
old, abandoned—"

When the energy wave hit, Val staggered back, words
frozen in her throat. She heard vampires screaming up
and down the street. Geoff was one of the screamers.
Char fell to the ground, curling up in a fetal ball.
Haven's hands clutched his temples, while Val stared
helplessly at them all. Lightning swirled through her
brain, leaving waves of nausea and confusion in its
wake.

"GoddessGoddessGoddess," she murmured, aware it
was both prayer and curse.

Then the light died—the flowing picture lights overhead, the casino signs, the shop lights, every light. Light
died.

Power surge, she realized, brought on by a different
kind of surge. Magic in the air. Loose in the city. Valentine stared into the natural darkness, hardly blind but not
used to the absence of artificial light in this modern
world. It was eerie, though it lasted only a few seconds.

The lights came back on, almost roaring back to life.
A momentary outage. No big deal to the mortal crowd.

There was a lot of noise, people loudly asking each other what had happened. Other sounds were buried in the crowd noise. But Valentine picked out every anomaly—feeling, smelling, and hearing every shout and scream. And the sweet scent of blood.

"Wake up!" she shouted at the Nighthawk children and the mortal man. She yanked Char to her feet. She shook Geoff to stop his screaming. All she had to give Haven was a stern look. "Calm down," she ordered them. "We've got big trouble." She looked around, and pointed. Shadows and strange shapes stalked across the landscape. Monsters moved among the huge herd of mortal sheep. "There. There. There. Go," she commanded the Nighthawks and the human hunter. "Take them down."

Chapter 16

IT WAS HARD to scream with his face turned into a fang-filled muzzle, but he managed to roar. It was impossible to cry. His vision was sharper, sensing light, shadow, and color in a way that was almost tactile. His hearing was sharpened, the range of sound much broader. Adrenaline pumped through him. And hunger was a spiritual need. Smell was enhanced, the scent of familiar blood everywhere. Much of it wasn't blood anymore, but ash, residue, a by-product that stank of evil.

He understood evil. He kind of liked it. But this—

Clare had died at the whim of evil. She'd died to call up evil. Her death had been—an ingredient—in a spell. Nothing more or less.

Ben shuddered, and retched, the taste of vomit hideous to the highly sensitive taste buds in his Hunter's mouth.

The memory of evil tickled at his mind. He could barely breathe, his lungs wanting to reject the charged, heated air. He had to get out of here. He had to get himself under control. He didn't know how or why he'd changed shape. Maybe it had been an instinctive reaction to the darkness and the pain. Maybe a protection against the magic, or a by-product of it. Didn't matter. He had to pull himself together.

He tried to change back.

All that did was send him howling in agony again. Thoughts tried to flee away from the pain, but Ben held on to himself, even inside this shape where it was all right to lose control and simply *be* the hungry nightmare beast that dwelled in every human soul.

"Monster."

The voice cut through the heat and the pain, through the grief and fear. Ben concentrated on the voice, recognizing it. He'd loved that voice a few minutes ago. Now he used the voice as a chain that led him to the scent of meat fed by warm, rich blood. He'd loved the physical form wrapped around the heart that beat so strongly with excitement and triumph. Reese's body was hard muscled. It would be tough and chewy, but relatively low fat.

Ben ran his tongue over his fangs. His mouth watered with hunger. His claws throbbed with the need to tear into flesh. His cock was swollen with the stronger, true Hunter need, to take and dominate, to feed on fear as well as flesh.

"You're drooling. Disgusting animal." Reese's voice

dripped with more self-satisfied triumph than it did sarcasm. The winner taking the time to gloat.

Ben looked into Reese's face, and was almost blinded by the blaze of power that shot from the magician's eyes. He had to throw his arm over his eyes. Even then the brightness burned against his closed lids.

Reese chuckled, aware of Ben's pain. "You were going to make me into something like you, weren't you? Stupid creature. I was going to be *your* slave? I don't think so. You'll make a nice pet, though. I'll put you on exhibit. Let you feed on my enemies. Won't that be fun?"

Ben opened his eyes, concentrated, and managed to finally banish the images of Morgan Reese as potential meal or power source from his mind. He made himself see Reese as an ugly, arrogant murderer standing over another victim, gloating. Ben accepted the murderer, being one himself, and having faced down murderers all his mortal and immortal life. He didn't even mind the gloating. It was being a victim that was galling.

Reese looked at his watch. "Earlier than I thought," he said. "But I still have to go. Still have a show to do. One more show. Then maybe another tomorrow night. Maybe not. Tonight I'll use the real power on my audience. Some of them will belong to me by the time the show is done. I'll burrow my will into their puny brains and have the beginnings of an empire. If you're good, I'll feed one of them to you." He smiled at Ben with the pride of possession. "I'm looking forward to seeing how your kind kills."

With that he turned and walked away. Ben looked after Reese, thinking, *You'll find out soon enough.*

When the door closed behind Morgan, Ben made himself look around, looking for a way out of the cage. It glowed now, with an icy blue light. Reese's spell had increased the magical strength he'd already conferred on the flimsy stage prop bars. Ben couldn't touch the bars. Beyond the cage, the room was growing hotter. Clare's body was no more than a husk drained of every bit of the vibrant energy that had made her what she was. Reese had consumed her to work his spell. And the red jewel he used in the ritual was resting on the marble table again. It glowed like a piece of burning coal, and something evil writhed beneath the burning surface. It gave off very bad vibes. Ben didn't know what Reese had done to the gem, but Ben didn't want it anywhere near him.

Damn. The man was good. But magic wasn't all it was cracked up to be. The physical world was the place where a person could really get things done. Ben turned slowly in the small cage, looking for a physical means of escape. He looked down at the cage floor. For some reason the prop was set on a slab of concrete. The material was cool and rough beneath his feet. He scraped the claws of one foot over the surface, and felt a monster's smile bare his fangs. Ben dropped to his knees, and scrabbled his front claws into concrete. It cracked and crumpled as he dug. Making a hole deep enough to squeeze through wasn't going to be the quickest way out of the cage, but it would do.

At least he didn't think it was going to be fast work. Not until he heard the crackling, cracking sounds coming from across the room. He looked up from his work, and what he saw sent a bolt of terror through him. He had to get out! He had to get out now!

It was amazing how fast you can work when a creature from hell is being born only a few feet away.

For a while Eddie just ran. No direction in mind, no purpose other than staying alive. Or so he thought. He didn't know when it occurred to him that he was running toward something, someone, but when he realized it, he came to a stop. Wolves howled at his back. The wolves were his brothers.

He threw back his head and laughed until his throat hurt.

"Brothers? What the fuck is that about?"

He hadn't thought like that in—centuries. Somebody had told him that once. Somebody who believed there was a community among their damned kind. Someone who protected.

"Mother," he whispered, rough-voiced, with panic rising again. It was too dark out on the city streets. The world was full of headlights and traffic lights and blaring horns borne on the strong, hot desert wind. And vampires.

Duke was coming after him, he was sure of it. The Nighthawk gone mad was going to seek out the strongest blood, a brother's blood. Duke could smell the secret inside him, Eddie was sure of it. Maybe he was one of the weak ones, one of the ones that never turned, but Nighthawk he was. It was going to get him eaten alive if he didn't find safety soon.

Eddie needed the lights.

He needed his mother. Valentine, who'd been in his dreams. More than his dreams. He'd seen her. He'd seen her. On a night like this, in the street. A scream of brakes. Horns. Like now. Shouts.

"Damn it, Eddie! Are you trying to get killed?"

"No," he answered the memory. "Trying to live. Help me." Eddie closed his eyes and shouted the thought across the centuries-old connection. *Mommy! Valentine! Lady and Mother—*

What? came back the annoyed mental shout.

Help me!

Oh, for Goddess's sake. I'm busy!

Eddie was used to ignoring people being irritated at him. He hadn't survived by showing pride, or giving up. And he knew his Val, knew what she cared about, what to bargain with. He sent her a mental picture of what had happened in the lab.

The answer he got was a mental gasp. And, *Get your skinny ass to Fremont Street right now!*

That was fine with Eddie. That was where he liked to spend his evenings anyway.

This was not how Haven had expected to spend the evening. He didn't mind. Martina's nest could wait. This was still a monster mash. Monsters were monsters, and killing them was what he was good at. But he didn't like that there were innocent civilians around. It wasn't just the vampires that were dangerous to the people in the street. Hunting down the vampires could make for some serious collateral damage. He most definitely didn't want that. He'd killed a few innocents in his time, and made a vow never to do it again.

He wasn't sure if it was a good or bad thing that most of the people on the street weren't aware they were in danger. The power outage had spooked people, but they were laughing about it as soon as the lights came on. When the monsters started running through the crowd, many assumed that they were costumed performers chasing other actors who were their "victims." It made much more sense to believe it was all part of some performance art show than to believe the monsters were real. Nobody thought, *The vampires are coming! The vampires are coming!*

Partly, Haven supposed, because a hunting vampire didn't look like the popular image of vampires, not even the ones in the Nosferatu movies. There was an animal appearance to what strigoi called the hunting mask. All the better to rend, rip, and tear. When they hunted, they didn't want to sip your blood and make you into either Mina or Renfrew.

Haven's real problem was knowing that hunting vampires were damned hard to kill.

He needed help, and not the Nighthawk trio currently patrolling the street. Haven didn't know what the magic ray was that turned the local vampires lethal, but he didn't trust it not to hit again. He couldn't afford to trust that the next time it wouldn't affect Valentine, Sterling, and even Char.

He moved away from the street, put his back against the wall of a building. He kept his gaze alertly on the action before him when he pulled out his cell phone and pressed a speed-dial number.

"Baker," he said when his partner picked up on the first ring. "You still want to kill vampires? There's a party on Fremont Street. Get Santini out of bed, and bring all your equipment. I've got stuff in the Jeep, but I have to get to the parking garage. Hurry."

He put the phone away, and became aware of Char by his side as she stepped out of shadows, still in human form, but her eyes were glowing. She was royally pissed. "What are you doing?" she demanded.

"Calling for reinforcements," was the simple answer.

"You can't call in Baker and Santini. The three of you can't kill real vampires."

Haven pointed to the crowd. "Somebody has to."

"We don't have to kill them," she insisted.

"Why not?" Sterling asked, appearing on Haven's other side. The male Nighthawk radiated excitement. He grinned maniacally.

"They're attacking humans," Haven pointed out.

"It's not their fault," Char argued. "Something changed them. They can't change back."

"We don't know that," Sterling argued. "Let's take them out."

"You sound like you want to hunt for fun."

"I'm a Nighthawk," he countered.

"Well, I'm an Enforcer. We have to round them up and keep them safe until they can change back. I do not kill the innocent."

"The people in the street are innocent," Haven pointed out. "I defend mortals."

"You can't bring Santini and Baker into this."

"We need the help."

"I won't let them kill my people."

They'd had conversations like this before. Haven had an answer for her. "Vampires aren't the only supernaturals in town, are they? Bound to be werewolves and fairies, fallens and demons hanging out in Vegas. Think that magic ray didn't affect them? You need us on patrol."

"Good point," Valentine said as she came up, dragging a skinny, scraggly-looking vampire with her. The skinny vampire was hunched over and looked scared to death, but he held an awesomely large rifle clutched to his chest. "This is Eddie," Valentine said, and patted him on the head. "An old boyfriend."

Char looked the newcomer over distastefully, and made a face at Valentine. "Yuck," was her judgment.

"It was the fourteenth century," Valentine answered. "You had to be there." She took a quick look at the street. "Talk quick, Eddie. We have work to do."

Eddie looked around, furtive and frantic. Haven saw that the vampire was dying for the lights, but Eddie was too scared to give in to his addiction. "Duke's coming," he said. "Berserk mode. He wants our blood. Wants my blood."

"What's he talking about?" Sterling questioned.

Haven had no trouble interpreting what the neon junkie meant. "The Enforcer of the City's gone off like the other crazy vamps. He's heading this way." He focused on Valentine. "You going to stop him? And how are you going to stop more magic from pouring out of that hotel of yours?" Haven had no doubt the origin of the spell that had transformed the monsters was the Silk Road. He didn't know if the current situation was some part of Martina's plan, but he was sure something more was coming. He didn't normally have premonitions, but the reality of impending doom tickled in his mind, and set his skin crawling.

Char put a hand on his arm. "I feel it too," she whispered to him. "Something wicked this way comes."

"It's not my hotel," Valentine countered. "All right, I own some stock, but I have no idea what's going on there."

"Maybe somebody better find out."

She nodded to Haven. Then she looked at her troops. "All right, boys and girls. Change of plans. Eddie, give Geoffrey the gun. I mean it," she ordered, and the scraggly vampire reluctantly replied. "Your friends will be here soon, Mr. Haven?" He nodded. "They have any experience in killing vampires?"

"No!" Char protested.

"It's necessary," Valentine replied.

"We've worked out some drills," Haven told Valentine.

"Jebel!"

"Hush, Charlotte."

"But—"

Valentine gave Char a stern look. "Char, you and Ge-off have to save the city from Duke. Only Nighthawks are going to be able to take out another Nighthawk. It's going to take both of you. That's your job. Do you understand me?"

Char bit her lower lip, and her eyes flashed fury, but she gave a tight nod. "Understood."

"Good. Now, Haven," Valentine said, concentrating on him. "I heard you say something about a Jeep."

"What do you need it for?" Haven asked.

"To stop the next wave of magic, of course. Come along. You and I are going to the Silk Road."

Haven didn't know why he didn't argue with this high-handed woman. He didn't know why he didn't question her plans and decisions. He was needed here. He didn't want to drive her to the hotel. She was already moving away from the other vampires. All he could do was dig out his car keys and hurry after.

Chapter 17

"So," GEOFF WONDERED as he and Char proceeded cautiously toward the entrance of the street. "How do you kill a Nighthawk?"

They'd waited for the mortal hunters to show up before starting this little jaunt. Geoff didn't like the idea of having Haven's buddies take over Nighthawk duties, but he did like the idea of having a few minutes alone with Char. Besides, Char had insisted that they herd rather than kill. Geoff wondered if the mortals would listen to her, but was happy not to have to hang around to watch their backs. Finding and containing the Enforcer of the City sounded like it was going to be a lot more fun. Though it was a daunting prospect as well.

He was aware of a large shadow moving in the darkness beyond the casino lights. He was in no hurry to confront this shadow. Not without a plan of some sort first. He almost wished he hadn't left the heavy-duty rifle behind with Eddie, but the neon junkie had had a fit about needing the protection. Char peered into the night up ahead. Her steps were as slow and cautious as his.

"My personal preference would be to call in Istvan," was her answer. "He's the *dhamphir.* I think he's the only one with the—equipment—for the job."

"Balls of steel?" Geoff wondered.

All he'd heard about the Enforcers' Enforcer was rumors. He'd seen the results of the *dhamphir*'s work, of course, when the nests were cleaned out in Seattle. There'd been a lot of heart-free bodies lying around. But none of the executed vampires Geoff had seen had been Nighthawks. If the Enforcer of the City had disappeared, it was probable that Istvan was the cause.

"You know this legend personally? More importantly, do you have his cell number?"

"Sort of," Char answered. "And he was in Chicago the last I heard. Doubt he could make it here in the next few minutes."

"Too bad. Is he good in bed?"

"What?"

He laughed as she stopped and turned to glare at him. It annoyed him that she always chose not to recognize when he was teasing. "I see you don't know."

"Of course not. We do not have sex with our own kind."

"Which is stupid if you think about it. Not only stupid, but disgusting."

"Not committing incest is disgusting? You're sick, Sterling."

"You liked kissing me."

"We aren't talking about that."

At least she didn't deny enjoying the kiss. "The point is," Geoff went on, "sleeping with mortals is what's wrong. Never mind incest, isn't our kind's having sex with a lower form of life what's really sick? Maybe taking mortal companions is supposed to be some kind of punishment for our original sin. Do you believe we should be punished for some mythological wrongdoing by the first vampires? What's that got to do with us?"

"This is no time to argue philosophy. Besides, if we don't take companions, how can we make other vampires?"

"Has anyone tried the old-fashioned method in the last few thousand years?"

"Vampires can't have babies."

"But we aren't vampires. Maybe Nighthawks can reproduce biologically instead of magically." He took her arm and turned her toward him. "You want to give it a try?"

"I want to kill a Nighthawk tonight," she said. "And not necessarily Duke."

Geoff was undeterred by her animosity. "Besides, there wouldn't be any incest involved."

Shock radiated from her like sonar waves. "We were both made by Jimmy Bluecorn!"

Jimmy had really made an impression on the girl. "Made vampires by Jimmy," Geoff clarified. "But not

Nighthawks. Jimmy didn't see you through the change
to Nighthawk, now did he?"

"No, but—"

"Valentine is my bloodmother. Fond as I am of her,
and hot as she is, I wouldn't dream of having sex with
her. That would be *yucky*." Char looked confused, and
he could tell that he'd finally said something that had
gotten through to her.

"I—" she began.

But the screaming coming toward them with the force
of a freight train cut her off. The conversation was
abruptly interrupted as the evening's crisis intruded
once more.

Geoff heard the pounding of footsteps under the
screams. At least two people were coming toward them.
The screaming woman's fear perfumed the air, and the
hunger radiating from the vampire turned the night grim
and ugly. Geoff had seen an innocent woman killed by
vampires once. There was something inside him that
wouldn't let it happen again.

"The innocent are not strigoi prey," Char said, pluck-
ing the thought from Geoff's mind.

He and Char shared a quick glance, and then moved
to put themselves between the woman and what hunted
her. Geoff could smell the sickness of the hunt-changed
female that came toward them. Unlike Char, her illness
and what had been forced on her didn't stir any compassion in him.

"Nobody ever gave me a silver knife," Geoff told
Char. "What do I do?"

"Fangs and claws," she answered, crouching, changing. "Fangs and claws."

Geoff concentrated on the fangs, the claws all right, not his own, but the ones coming toward him. And on the glowing beast's eyes full of cunning and hunger. It was a mistake to meet the creature's eyes.

Hunger flashed between them. Hot desire—for blood, for sex, for meat. "Yours," Geoff said, the memory of Moira's death blocking the baser needs that called to him.

The mortal woman between the Nighthawks and the vampire stopped screaming. Geoff didn't know if she saw him and Char or not. What she did was fall to the ground, and roll, getting out of the way.

The vampire started to lunge after her. Char sprang forward. Geoff was less than a heartbeat behind her. They struck in unison, claws and fangs. It was the vampire's turn to scream. Char's claws dug through flesh, and ribs. Geoff came in through the vampire's spine. Bones cracked loudly. He and Char's hands closed together around a beating heart. Their gazes met over the body, eyes glowing with hunter's fire.

After you, Geoff thought at his hunting partner, and loosed his hold.

Char didn't act the lady. She let him back off from the body. She took the heart out of it, and let the dead creature drop at her feet. It was the sexiest move Geoff had ever seen.

She didn't eat the heart, but squeezed it hard in her fist. Blood pumped out, staining the sidewalk and walls to either side. It covered Char's clothes, and she held an arm over her face to keep the blood off her muzzle and out of her eyes. She held on to the heart until it stopped beating, then threw it away in a hard lob that bounced the dead muscle off a wall and into the gutter.

Geoff licked his lips, wanting to taste the hot blood and heart meat, but he understood why Char didn't consume the prize. The creature had been a neon junkie to begin with, then changed helplessly into hunting form by magic. Why take even a faint risk of infection for a snack?

He wanted to taste her too, to lick the blood off her face, and the black shirt that didn't show the red stains, and to mate. He loved the way she reacted with merciless instinct when the time came to act. She was a woman of compassion and a stone killer all at once. Damn, that was hot!

Char changed back into human form with such speed that Geoff had trouble following it. Not all that practiced in the transformation, it took him a long moment of hard concentration to change back, and it hurt a little.

"Damn," he muttered when he had a mouth that could form words again.

He looked around for Char, and saw her starting to kneel by the hunched form of the mortal woman. The woman sat up as Char knelt, and everyone's attention was drawn to the mortal man dressed in black leather who ran silently up to them from the direction of the chase.

"Della?" the newcomer called. He rushed up to the woman. "Baby, you okay?"

"Santini?" Char asked, jumping to her feet. "Santini?"

"You're late!" Della shouted, letting Santini help her up. Once on her feet, she smacked him on the shoulder. "That was *not* how the plan was supposed to go!"

"Got tackled by a fairy—or something," Santini explained to his angry bride. "Baker had to drive the bastard off with a flamethrower." He talked as he patted her down, brushed her off. "You're okay, right? No bites?"

"I've been bitten plenty of times," the former companion reminded her husband. "But not by that loser." Della turned to look at Geoff and Char. "Thanks."

Char angrily faced the mortals. "What the hell were you doing? Using Della as bait?"

"Yep," Santini replied. "Second time in the last half hour. Sorry it didn't come off like clockwork this time, baby."

Della's anger at her mate seemed to have passed. She patted his bearded cheek. "At least I'm okay. It's a good plan."

"Gotta go," Santini said to Geoff and Char. "Can't leave Baker holding the fort." He took Della's hand and they started back the way they'd come. "Thanks for the help," he called as they left.

Geoff looked down at the dead vampire, mind racing. The critter had been set up, trapped. Not a bad idea.

"Bait," Geoff said thoughtfully. He glanced over his shoulder, into the darkness where the city's Enforcer wandered, hunted. Geoff could feel the bespelled Nighthawk's searching hunger. He wasn't looking for just any victim. The need in Duke was specific. Not for Chinese, or for pizza, but for—

"A Nighthawk," Char said, grabbing Geoff's arm. "He wants a Nighthawk."

Geoff smiled slowly. "We can give him one."

"Bait," Char agreed.

"Eddie," they said together.

Ice flayed the skin off Ben's back as he crawled out of the cage, but he accepted the pain for the chance to get to freedom. Besides, the vicious cold almost felt good in the rising temperature of the room. It was raining in the room now, and steam was rising. He had to get out. He had to get out now. Rain wasn't going to save him.

He thought he could save himself. Thought he knew how, when he could think at all—'cause his brain was trying to go away. Animal easier. The longer he was in beast shape, the more beast he became. *Smart beast,* he told himself. *Remember you're a smart beast. Try to be.*

He had to get to Reese. Magic was in Reese. Magic had to die. Reese had to die.

Despite the fear, despite the pain, Ben smiled at that. Hunter's mask wasn't made to smile, but the snarl that pulled at his muzzle would do.

He wanted, needed to run once he'd managed to crawl out from under the bottom of the cage. Tough as his skin was, his hands were shredded. Broken claws were growing back, and the regeneration brought nothing but more pain.

The monster was crying now, making sharp, mewling sounds. Ben couldn't look at the thing, not when it was growing out of Clare's disintegrating body. The stench of her burning was still in the air. Fire flickered on the edge of Ben's enhanced peripheral vision. He was going to burn too, if he didn't get out soon.

Animal mind wanted to run. Beast said running was the only way to survive. He could outrun anything.

Not this. Not this.

He was beast, but he wasn't the monster here.

He crawled, crawled. Get to Reese. Get to door. Then get to Reese. Inch, inch, inch. Rain poured onto his back. Water ran beneath hands and knees. Water was rising to a boil. Burning. Fire and water and air burning.

Ben found the door. He hadn't believed he would. He had to stand then, with that thing at his back.

Ben made a picture of Clare form in the beast's mind. He made the beast remember the taste of blood. Hunger for Reese's blood.

Even fear of the monster couldn't stop the need for blood. Need for revenge. Need for freedom.

He rose out of the boiling water, prayed the scalding steam would hide him. He found the doorknob. Claws made it harder, but he turned it. He jerked so hard the door came off its hinges. Ben fell forward, water pouring out into the hall with him. There were more sprinklers going off out here. An alarm sounded in the

distance. Fire alarm, Ben recognized the sound. Sprinklers spraying water. Automatic systems doing their job.
Where were people? Where security? Cameras everywhere. Who watching? Clare? Clare was gone.

Companions, then? Nest members? Slaves? Where
were his crew? They were charged with protecting this
place.

Reese, he remembered. Reese's magic. Reese must
have hurt all of them. Now the place was on fire.

Monster's doing. Monster would kill all.

But the beast would kill Reese first. Make up for having started it all.

Back in the dressing room, the monster screamed.

In the hall, the beast scrambled to his feet and ran.

"Do you know anything about vampire history, Mr.
Haven?"

Haven already knew that no matter how he answered
Valentine's question, he was in for a lecture. It seemed
like every woman he met was a talker. Was there something about his aura that—

"Projects that you're a good listener," Valentine finished the thought for him.

Haven took his concentration off weaving through the
heavy traffic long enough to give Valentine a dirty look.

"You strong, silent types make us girls want to con-
fide in you."

"Nah," he answered. "I think it's because I've started
hanging with geeks."

She smiled, her dark eyes glowing. When Char showed off her vampire side, he always found it at least a bit disturbing. But from Valentine it was kind of cute. He had the feeling that she had to make an effort to act like a vampire.

"I'm old," she explained to him. "It becomes less important. At least, the urgency dies down to a mostly manageable level."

"Mostly?"

"I'm not dead yet. Now, where was I?"

Haven didn't answer. His driving was automatic now. Most of his attention was on the Silk Road as they approached it. Invisible energy pulsed and twined around the huge building's many spires and domes. It was like he saw the place through a kind of midnight heat haze. And the haze was spreading.

"Don't like the look of it," he said.

"And there's a black-hearted feel to it as well," the old vampire added. "Black magic. I hate black magic."

Haven canted an eyebrow at her. "Don't vampires come from black magic?" Oh, God, he thought. Now I've done it. There was no one to blame now but himself if Valentine went off on the lecture circuit.

"Yes," she answered. "We were created by an act of evil. The first vampires brought it all on themselves."

"Really," he said in a tone he hoped would convey, *Please don't say any more.*

It didn't stop her. "There used to be a lot more magic in the world, Haven. A whole lot. Magic is energy."

"Yeah. I know that."

"You know how astronomers say that the universe is made up of stuff created during the Big Bang?"

"I try not to watch the Discovery Channel."

"There's stuff they know a little about, like gravity and matter and—stuff. But there's all this energy they can't find. Dark matter, I think they call it. I think magic's part of what the universe is made of. It exists, but it's dissipating. Or maybe there just aren't as many sentient beings around these days who can use it."

"Seems like you vampires might be responsible for some of that."

"Maybe," she agreed. "But in the old days most people had access to some kind of magical sensitivity. Many people were so powerful that they were acknowledged as gods. There was a goddess who lived among a nomadic people, a very long time ago. She was immortal—always young, always beautiful. She found a way to share her immortality with her people. Every decade or so there would be a gathering of her whole tribe. During a secret ceremony she would open her veins and let her blood flow into an elixir she made out of herbs and wine. Then her priests and priestesses would pass chalices of this sacred wine among the people. The elixir added to their lifespan, cured sickness. It was a great gift from the goddess to the people she loved. But people are stupid, selfish, and incredibly greedy."

"That's the truth," Haven agreed. They were sitting at a stoplight. He would have run it, but they were in a center lane, surrounded by far too many cars for the Jeep to clear. "Why are we driving to the hotel?" he asked Valentine. "You could have gotten there on your own power long before now."

"I've never taken up the vampire sport of running," she answered. "Besides, I need to be in an enclosed space for a while." She touched the door frame and ran a hand across the passenger side window. "Flimsy as this box of metal and glass is, I find being inside walls comforting. It's a rough night, you don't want me getting panicky on you."

"Point taken," he told her. "That why you need to talk so much? To help keep it together?"

"Yes."

The light changed and he pressed down on the gas. "Then keep talking, sister."

"All right. How much further?"

Haven squinted, concentrated hard on the street. "Hard to tell. It keeps seeming farther away—then closer. Like a mirage. And don't tell me that we've already passed the Mirage."

"I did notice the volcano going off as we drove by. Don't you love the surrealistic nature of this town? About the Goddess," Valentine went on.

Haven noticed the glint of a small silver pendant hanging on a chain around Valentine's neck, resting just above the V-neck of her black dress. The pendant was a tiny figure of a bare-breasted woman in a long belled skirt. The woman was holding a pair of snakes. Valentine touched the figure when she noticed him looking. "That the vampire goddess?" he asked.

"No," she answered. "The Lady of Snakes is someone else's goddess. To continue the vampire goddess's tale, somebody in her priesthood came up with a truly stupid idea. Not satisfied with a long, healthy life, the priests decided they wanted to be immortal too. So, they figured that if drinking a few drops of the goddess's blood was so beneficial, imagine what consuming the goddess would do for them. They decided to kill and eat her."

Haven didn't shock easily, but this rattled him. "How do you kill a goddess?" he asked.

"Very good question. One this ancient priesthood apparently didn't consider. What they did involved the darkest form of magic. They had a lot of power between them, and used it to bespell specially forged silver daggers."

"That's where the Enforcer blades come from?"

"I suppose the traditional weapon of the Enforcers comes from the old legends," she answered. "The priesthood used their magic knives to kill the goddess. They drank her blood, ate her flesh. Reveled in the lust of killing."

"Then they turned into vampires."

"Not yet. I bet you were a bugger to tell bedtime stories too."

Haven could not recall anyone ever having told him bedtime stories. He had not had that kind of a childhood. "Go on," he told Valentine.

"Goddesses cannot be killed," she said. "Not even by the darkest of black magic. But they can be pissed off."

"I bet."

"This goddess returned from the supposed dead and laid a curse on her rebellious followers."

"That's when they became vampires?"

"Yes. Instead of granting them the gift of immortality, she turned immortality into a curse. They were banished from the daylight. Sunlight was a gift for the mortal world. They were given the constant hunger to hunt and kill the mortals they could not dwell among. They must take lovers that they could not keep. Having your heart constantly broken is part of the curse." She sighed. "Anyway, that's how vampires came to be."

"Okay." He finally came to the entrance to the hotel grounds he'd been looking for. "How do Nighthawks come into all this?" He bypassed the front entrance to the Silk Road and pulled into the parking garage.

As he pulled into a parking spot, Valentine answered, "That, Mr. Haven, is another story."

They didn't have time for more stories. They got out of the Jeep and Haven opened up the back. He opened up the locked metal case where he kept his weapons stash.

"Impressive," Valentine commented as he gathered equipment.

"Thanks. You want any of this?" he questioned as he loaded concealed pockets and strapped on an equipment belt.

"No, thanks."

"Fine." He shut the case, and slammed the rear door. He paused for a moment, and something that was not fear, but was frighteningly disturbing, rushed like wild-

fire all the way through him. He let the reaction pass—
made it pass.

He looked at Valentine. "Ready to rock?"

She didn't look all that confident herself, but she did
smile at him, with an impressive amount of fang showing. "Let's go."

Chapter 18

"SOMETHING'S WRONG."

Haven gave her a wry look, but Valentine could tell he felt it too. There was more than residue and potential magic in the air. There was more than the humming, harsh energy spun off by hordes of gamblers in the casino. There was more than the uneven, tinkling music of the slot machines.

"It's hot," she said.

He stood very still for a moment, then nodded slowly. "Air-conditioning's working hard to compensate. Heat a by-product of the magic?"

"Good thought."

They were standing in the center of the lobby, beneath a dome beautifully painted to show the night sky. Mortals were all around them, going about their business. They stood by the front desk, gathered in the furniture groupings set under draping silk canopies. She could detect mortals everywhere, in their rooms, the casinos, the bars, the restaurants, the spas and shops, in the kitchens and corridors. She detected dormant and injured energy coming from the cash vault, the money cages, the security centers. Not a vampire was stirring, which at least meant that she and Haven wouldn't have to fight off any crazed hunting vampires while they sought out the real source of trouble.

Too many of the underneath world worked in the hotel, she thought. This kept the place secure from mortal attack. It would likely stop another vampire incursion as well. It was proving horrifically vulnerable in the face of a magical assault.

"Where's Ibis?" Valentine wondered, searching for the psychic signature of a strong, ancient vampire. Nothing. Why wasn't he here to protect his people?

"What are we waiting for?" Haven interrupted her mental search.

She brought her focus back to the tough mortal. "Patience is not your strong point, is it?"

"Is it yours?" was his reply.

"No," she had to admit. She'd always been too impulsive.

"Where to?" he asked.

"Give me a second." Valentine concentrated on finding the strongest source of magic, hunting through layers and waves of energy. Mortal emotions, vampire energy signatures. She encountered all sorts of scents and gradations. "Three sources," she finally told Haven.

"You've been here before?" He nodded. "Good. Tell me what you know." She pointed in one direction.

"Vampire museum is that way," he answered.

"Okay. What's coming from there is mostly latent stuff. Not a threat zone, then." She pointed again.

"Uh, saw video screens on this area. Storage rooms, dressing room, I think. The stage magician's place."

"Heat source coming from there," Valentine said. She shuddered as she drew her mind away from the energy. Heat raced up her skin. She pushed away suspicion for now. "We're going to have to check that out."

She concentrated on the third source of magic, pointed again. There was shielding around this source, but full of pinprick holes that let power leak out.

"Theater," Haven said. "Magic show in there."

"Real magic show tonight," she answered. "Real magician. He's weaving spells. I think we've found the cause of the trouble."

Haven's dark eyes suddenly lit with excitement. "Yes! I should have figured this out already. It's the magician. The vampire gave the spell book to the magician." He looked totally disgusted. "I'm an idiot. Murphy wanted to get the book back from him, but I didn't think it was important."

Valentine remembered there'd been mention of translated spells as well as the scrolls when Haven told them about Martina's plot against the Enforcers. "I thought Martina had the translations."

"I was there when a vampire gave the spell book to the human magician. Reese. The guy who does his act here in the hotel."

"Why would a vampire give up a spell book?"

"It had something to do with sex," Haven answered. "Gifts to a new boyfriend. It was stuff taken from the museum. There was the book, a gold cup, and—"

Valentine watched as the mortal's deeply tanned skin went pale. "What else?" she demanded, deeply worried by this fearless man's startling reaction.

"There was a gemstone. Looked like a ruby. Murphy called it a dragon's egg. Said it's used in alchemy."

Valentine felt her knees go weak. She would have very much liked to sit down. Or better yet, run away. Her throat constricted with momentary panic. Then she managed to say. "Dragon's egg. Oh. Fucking. Shit."

We are so screwed, she thought. *If it's real. But it can't be real, because Ibis is not a fool. He couldn't possibly have put out a—*

"What is it?"

"Come with me," she said, and marched in the direction of the theater.

They cut through the casino, and wove through heavy foot traffic in a shopping mall designed to look like an exotic bazaar, with narrow lanes and closely packed vendors' stalls. Beyond the mall three corridors met in a wide open area before the theater entrance. Valentine paused before the theater doors and rubbed her chin.

"Getting hotter," Haven commented.

She nodded. She could hear water running in the distance, and didn't think it had anything to do with decorative fountains. She glanced toward the hallway on their right. The heat was coming from that way. And something that gave her a very bad feeling.

"What if the place is on fire?" she questioned. "Wouldn't there be alarms going off? Sprinkler systems working? The fire department notified?"

Haven followed her gaze, with noticeable reluctance. "Emergency systems are likely set up in sectors. The hotel's huge, makes sense that alarms would only go off in the trouble spot. Everything would be monitored in the control center."

Valentine balled her fists in frustration. "And the command center is currently manned by unconscious nest members." There was magic swirling and building behind the closed theater doors, and it wasn't nice. There was magic coming from down that hall. And—

"Smoke," Haven said.

Valentine sniffed. The smoke was invisible, but it was there. "The place is on fire."

"I figured that out."

People were all around them. "Nobody else knows. We have to get everyone out of here."

"We?"

"You're right," she said, whirling toward the theater doors. She looked over her shoulder at Haven. "You sound the alarm. I'll take care of the mortal sorcerer."

"But—! God damn it!" He pulled a sawed-off shot-gun out from under his coat. He aimed toward the ceiling and fired. "All right, people!" he shouted over the sudden screaming. "Listen up!"

Well, that got everyone's attention. This was not necessarily a method meant to stave off panic, but Valentine
left Jebel Haven to deal with the emergency in his own
way. She moved to the doors, and slipped inside the
darkened auditorium.

"Look at me! Look at me!"

Ben followed the voice. The hunt hunger was growing.
That should have made him sharper, but—Reese—the
voice up ahead—Reese twisted him. Made the hunger—
the beast's—his—enemy. Couldn't think and be beast.
The closer he got to Reese—the harder it was to think.

Part of the spell? A way Reese had of controlling him?

Ben was too stubborn for that. He moved slowly, like
swimming through hot tar, but he moved. Moved down
halls, through doors, around backstage props. Reese had
two assistants. Had. They'd seen Ben. Tried to run. Tried
to warn Reese. But Ben was fast. He hadn't felt them die,
but they wouldn't be getting up for a while. Wouldn't be
warning anyone that beasts were roaming the world.

Reese wasn't missing them. He wasn't doing stage
magic tonight. Ben could feel the power gathering. Maybe
that was what was sucking the life—the smarts—out of
him. Even if he went mad, or lost every grain of intelligence, he was going to get his prey.

Had to—save the fucking day.

He got closer to Reese, one step at a time. Now he
could hear the voice.

The voice was saying, "Listen to my voice. Look into
my eyes. Let go. Lose yourself. Lose yourself in me."

For a moment Ben was caught by the soothing murmur, felt the lines of power snaking out, grasping for control. But he didn't stop moving forward, inch by slow inch, even in the moment of wanting to be seduced.

He was already Reese's prisoner. Not going to get in deeper. He could feel people out there beyond the stage lights, responding, listening, wanting.

Had to save the others from Reese.

He finally reached the back of the stage. Stepped onto it, into lights.

And knew Reese was waiting for him.

Reese turned and smiled, and waved him forward. A trap already set for the beast. A triumphant display of what Morgan Reese could do. Ben snarled. He put up a struggle, but he moved forward. Which was what he wanted to do anyway. Reese kept smiling, even if he was aware of Ben's fangs, and reaching claws.

Valentine put away her cell phone and finally turned her attention to the stage. She'd been aware of the sorcerer cajoling the audience that had come to see a magic show. He had a very nice, very persuasive voice, but she didn't pay attention to the words as she stood in the back of the dark theater making a quick call.

She was near the doors, but out of the way, and disgruntled people had been filing out in a steady stream past her the whole time she was on the phone. Many complained about Reese's failed attempt at mass hypnotism nonsense on their way out, grumbling that this was not what they'd paid to see. She didn't blame them for going. Hotel shows in Las Vegas were not cheap, and fake tricks were far more impressive to most people than the real shit the ugly guy on stage was pulling.

Running her gaze over the auditorium seats, she saw that maybe a dozen mortals were gazing fixedly at the sorcerer. These were the few with some psychic gifting. Other people were still in their seats, looking bored or suspicious, waiting for something *interesting* to happen. She considered that it might be best not to confront the sorcerer until she got all the mortals out of there.

"I suppose I could yell 'Fire!' " she murmured. And it would even be the truth.

She heard the voice droning on, but her attention wasn't drawn to the stage. A collective gasp went up from what few people were left in the audience. Looking at Morgan Reese, she saw that he'd decided to incorporate a vampire into his act.

The vampire was a big male, rather gloriously naked, with a full hunting hard-on.

Valentine couldn't help but smile. "Looks like the show just stopped being PG-13."

Taking a more dispassionate look at the vampire, she saw how hard the hunter fought against the mortal's control. This wasn't one of the poor junkies who'd been rendered mindless when the bolt of magic struck. This one retained intelligence. And he was totally pissed off at the mortal who thought he was the one in control.

"Arrogant, untrained, wanna-be wizard," she murmured. Trouble was, Reese did have control.

Enough to keep the hunter's fangs and claws at bay. He let the vampire take swipes at him, snap at him, and dodged and danced away. He made a show of humiliating the vampire, and the remainder of the audience applauded.

It was a dangerous game, and Valentine let it go on. She let the magician dance, and the vampire grovel. She wrapped shadows around herself, just a little. The magician didn't notice her moving up the center aisle toward the stage. The man was full of power, but too full of himself. He focused on putting on a show. She drew closer. Closer.

The magician was calling the vampire names now. He'd picked up a fake sword and stabbed and struck at the vampire. The vampire threw back his head and howled.

Reese laughed. And so did the audience.

Valentine stepped up on the stage, dropped shadows and psychic shielding to announce her presence in several ways, and said, "Hi, there."

Reese felt her presence as the blow she intended. He spun toward her, mouth gaping.

Behind Reese, the vampire howled again. And punched a hole through the mortal's chest from behind. Bone cracked, blood spurted, and Reese's open mouth screamed and screamed.

Reese lived long enough to be spun around, and see the vampire holding his beating heart in his bloodied claws. Valentine doubted if the overconfident mortal was still alive when the vampire began to eat the warm, red heart.

Valentine heard the screams and the stampede from the auditorium. She was glad she'd decided not to wait to get the audience out first, as letting them watch a hunter take prey was a good way of evacuating the place without having to explain the situation. She did watch to see if the vampire would go after the fleeing audience, but she didn't have to worry about stopping him.

As soon as he'd finished with the heart, he collapsed on top of the bloody body. Slowly, with far more effort than it should take, the vampire resumed human form. He lay on Reese for a few seconds, spent, shaking. Valentine waited.

When he looked up, he was crying. "He killed Clare," the vampire told Valentine. "Burned her to death. Used her to make magic."

Valentine was aware of the grief, and the self-recriminations. She guessed that Clare had been this vampire's companion. She guessed that Clare's last name was Murphy, and had been Haven's informant inside the hotel. And that this was the vampire Haven had seen giving Reese the spell book. So what had happened to the companion was this vampire's fault. She didn't point this out; the vampire already knew his crimes.

"You got even," she said. "We always do. Now." She bent down, avoided a pool of blood, and pulled the vampire off the cooling body. "Tell me how this bastard burned your Clare Murphy to death."

Chapter 19

IT WASN'T FAIR. It never was. Hadn't it been enough that he'd brought the warning? No. They'd betrayed him. Valentine had left him alone. Now these two had dragged him into a scheme that could get him killed. They were making him march through a dark parking lot toward the most frightening thing in this town. There were a few cars dotting the expanse of the lot. Eddie knew Duke could be hiding behind any one of them.

"I don't want to die," Eddie said. "I'm too old to die."

"You are *so* pathetic," the female Nighthawk complained.

The pair were walking behind him. They'd told him they were going to guard his back, but he doubted it.

"I was born pathetic. It's a valuable survival skill."

"Must be," the male said. "You're still around."

"Maybe we won't have to kill the Enforcer," the woman said.

She was pitiful. Eddie glanced furtively back at her. "He's crazy," Eddie said. "They've tortured him. Drugged him. He was dangerous even before the magic changed him."

While Eddie did not know this for a fact, he did know that he'd betrayed Duke to Martina's people. He was sure Duke knew it, and that Duke was coming after him.

"You have to kill him," he told the young Night-hawks. "To protect us all. And the mortals," he added slyly, knowing that the girl at least was interested in mortals' welfare.

Char wished she'd never answered Eddie's complaints. His voice was irritating, almost more than his attitude. She couldn't imagine how the lovely and mysterious Valentine could have once had him as a mortal lover.

Mortal lover. She thought about Jebel, who wanted to marry her, and smiled. Then she thought about Ster-ling's contention that there was a possibility that Nighthawks didn't need mortal lovers. Was that why she hadn't taken Jebel as a companion yet? Because she could love him without possessing him?

She glanced at Geoff Sterling, walking beside her. She should be keeping her full attention on the matter at hand. Sterling had stripped off his jacket, and his black shirt was unbuttoned, revealing a broad chest and a nice six-pack of abs. She was mostly certain that his flashing skin had nothing to do with his efforts to seduce her.

What she was certain of was that shifting into full

Nighthawk form was not something Sterling was used to. When the transformation happened, body mass didn't change, but shape did shift somewhat, bulk up. Wearing comfortably loose clothing came in handy. Personally, Char preferred wearing sweats while working, but the knit shirt and shorts she was wearing now did the job. She'd stashed her sandals in a huge flower container back on Fremont Street. She looked at Sterling's feet.

"You might want to ditch your shoes. Back claws come in handy."

After a moment's surprise, he gave her a sheepish grin. "Yeah. Forgot about that."

He stopped to slip off his shoes and socks. She waited with him, but kept her eyes on Eddie as the old vampire continued across the wide expanse of the lot. The parking lot covered a large area, and was bounded by busy streets on all four sides. The bright flash of headlights formed an almost solid wall of light around the place where they stood in darkness. The lot was adjacent to a fenced-off construction site of several acres. Char supposed this was the location for yet another hotel casino destination resort. As if the city needed more garish factories built to separate people from their money.

"You're being judgmental," Sterling said.

She jumped a little at the sound of his voice. "I'm allowed," she said.

"Hey!" Eddie called from up ahead. "You two paying attention?"

Sterling let out a hiss of anger. "Why can't he be quiet?"

Char assumed it was because the weasel was scared. She hurried to catch up with him, and left Sterling to watch her back, while she watched Eddie's.

"I don't like the dark," Eddie said when she had reached him. "I've never liked the dark."

She almost snapped that if he didn't like the dark, he shouldn't have become a vampire. But then, he hadn't been given a choice, had he? That was what it was like in the old days, vampires taking whomever they wanted, whenever they wanted.

Who was she kidding? Vampires were still allowed to take whomever they wanted. It was wrong, but it was the Law. It disturbed her that she could let herself admit that one of the Laws of the Blood was a mistake. It wasn't that she didn't occasionally entertain thoughts about right and wrong, it was just that now she could blame Sterling for making her question her beliefs. She didn't want to think that Geoff Sterling could influence her about anything.

Pay attention! It's dangerous out here!

Char wasn't sure if the thought had originated within herself, or if Eddie or Sterling had projected it at her. Wherever it came from, it was a necessary reminder.

Paying attention, Char took a slow look around, with all her senses on alert. Magic still drifted through the air, like smog. There were shadows all around, making black holes in the night. Flights coming and going from McCarran crisscrossed in front of the full moon and the spear of light stabbing up from the tip of the Luxor pyramid. The lights of the hotels blazed away in the distance, but out here it was all very mysterious, the darkness velvety and dense.

Geoff hung back and watched Char watch the night. There was a lot he could learn from her, even if she wasn't the most experienced Enforcer on the Council's payroll. From what he could figure out, she was more of a researcher than an active member of the force. He hadn't known the Enforcers did anything other than slay stray strigs and so-called Law breakers. Val had promised to teach him a few tricks whenever the urge to hunt came upon him. But since he hadn't felt any need to thin the strigoi herd since the night she'd brought him through the second rebirth, no instructions had been forthcoming.

Maybe it would be more fun to sign on as apprentice Hunter to Char. There was a lot they could teach each other. A lot of the psychic and magical world they could explore. For example, how was it they had met in midair over the daylight city? It had been a very different sort of astral projection from their meeting inside their heads last day. There was so much that vampires and Nighthawks were not taught about their abilities. Having had that taste of flying in the sunlight with Char, he wanted to learn what kind of power they really had. He felt there was a purpose in their being drawn together. All Geoff had to do was convince her to dump her mortal and come away with him. How hard could that be?

"Jebel," Char said, suddenly coming to a stop and lifting her head. Geoff felt the shudder of dread go

through her. She whirled around to face the Silk Road in
the far distance. "Jebel's in trouble. Something's going
to happen."

Geoff hurried up to Char, and Eddie backed away
from them. "He can take care of himself," Geoff reminded Char. "Focus."

"Yeah, focus," Eddie called from deep shadow.

Then Eddie screamed as Duke rushed toward him,
shedding shadow like a discarded cloak. Char transformed. Geoff shifted shape without even thinking
about it. Muscles rippled and bulked up, claws sprang
out, long, sharp, and deadly. His face transformed into a
hideous, heavy muzzle. Senses sharpened. It felt *good*.
It was a totally freeing experience.

Geoff growled, fought the urge to howl with pure joy.
And jumped when Eddie fired the heavy rifle at the attacking Nighthawk. The stench of burning flesh scented
the air. Duke yowled in pain. The noise of the rifle
blended with Duke's shout of rage. The Enforcer didn't
wait to be fired on again. He leapt at Eddie.

The old vampire backpedaled and tripped over his
own feet. Duke flew at him as he went down, flat on his
back on the potholed concrete. But Char was there, bar-
reling into Duke from the side. Duke spun to face her,
and they went at it, snapping and clawing. Geoff stared
in amazement for a moment.

Two Nighthawks fighting was a rare thing in their
world. Seeing a pair of equals go at it all fang and claw
and deadly speed was an amazing thing to experience.

Rage and hunger crackled out from them. Hearts thundered. Death waited.

Char clawed open Duke's back. Blood spurted and spattered the ground. Duke snapped at her shoulder. They rolled together across the parking lot.

Geoff ran forward. Nighthawk or not, that was also Char taking hits from a Nighthawk male much bigger than she was. He grabbed the huge rifle from Eddie, who still cowered on the ground. Geoff raced after the struggling pair, aware, but not caring, when Eddie jumped up behind him and fled away from the fight.

Geoff fumbled with the rifle, only to discover that in his current shape it was no good to him. The trigger hadn't been designed to accommodate his huge, Nighthawk claws. So he ran up to the fight. Duke was crouched over Char, snapping at her throat as she held him off, his fangs inches from her face. Geoff smashed the heavy weapon across the back of Duke's head.

It barely got the other Nighthawk's attention, but it was enough for Char to push Duke back a few inches. Geoff used the space to grab Duke around the neck and haul him all the way off of Char. Char rose to her knees, buried her claws in the tough flesh over Duke's heart. Geoff held Duke while he yowled and writhed. Then he buried his own muzzle in the back of Duke's neck, biting into Duke's spine. Geoff shook Duke like a terrier with a weasel, all the while savoring the taste of blood and bone in his mouth. Char went for Duke's heart. Duke screamed, and screamed, until the screaming abruptly stopped. Geoff and Char let the dead body drop at the same time.

Char had Duke's heart in her hands. She bit into it, then raised her muzzle and met Geoff's hungry gaze. For a moment he thought they were going to fight over the prize, and excitement at the possibility thrummed through him, hotter than lust.

Then Char tossed the other half of the Nighthawk's heart to him, and Geoff gulped down the prize, felt fresh power pump through him. This time Geoff did throw back his head and howl in joy.

"You sound like a werewolf," Char said, disapprovingly, as she turned back to her human form.

Geoff spent one more moment enjoying the victory before he took on his normal shape. "Don't insult me," he answered. They knelt on either side of Duke's body. Char was wiping her bloody hand's on Duke's shirt. "Don't tell me that wasn't fun for you?" Geoff questioned.

"Of course it was fun," she answered. She looked at him with deep disapproval. "I hate that it was fun."

"You're repressed."

"We just killed one of our own," she reminded Geoff. "I don't like the precedent." She looked around, as though searching for Eddie. "Neither of us could have done it alone. Or without Eddie's help."

"I guess he showed his Nighthawk roots."

"If Duke had been sane, it would have been even harder for us to take him down." She shrugged. "I'm not even sure killing Duke was necessary."

"He did attack Eddie."

"Maybe he had a right to."

"Maybe you shouldn't think so much. It's over and done." He looked around as well. For the first time ever he wondered about mortal interference. "There were gunshots, and screams. The cops might be on the way."

Char looked down at the body of the late Enforcer of the City. "I wonder where he dumped bodies?"

"It's a little late to ask him now."

She rose to her feet. Geoff followed. Her gaze was once more drawn to the Silk Road. "This is not my town," she said. "I've cleaned up enough of the mess already."

This did not sound like the dutiful young Enforcer, Char McCairn to Geoff. "Oh, really?" he asked.

"Really," she said. "Jebel needs me now." She took a deep breath. Without looking back at the dead body in the parking lot, she started to run.

Geoff, having no interest in cleaning up the mess either, said, "I've got your back," and followed.

Holding the shotgun up against his shoulder, Haven surveyed the nearly empty lobby with the satisfaction of a job well done. The satisfaction didn't alleviate the sense of impending disaster that haunted the back of his mind, but it was something. He doubted the hotel was completely cleared out, but alarms were sounding and he'd made sure the fire department was notified. He'd done as much as he could, scaring the hell out of a few folks in the process. All in all, it was the best time he'd had since the underground parking garage firefight in Chicago a couple of weeks ago.

"Always the man of action, aren't you, Mr. Haven?"

"Damn right," he answered Valentine. He caught a whiff of burnt hair as he turned around.

Valentine shook gray ash off the ends of her dark curls. "Got a little too close," she said. "But I had to make sure of what I was looking at. We are in such trouble." She sounded casual.

"You've got the cool attitude down cold, lady," he complimented the old vampire. "But there's fear in your eyes."

"Yes, well." She surveyed the deserted lobby while she ran fingers through her hair, shaking loose more ash. "Shakespeare," she said. "Or Ray Bradbury. Take your pick."

He scowled. "What?"

"Something wicked this way comes, my dear."

"How wicked?" he asked. "Which way?"

"About as wicked as they come. It wants out. Its wings are still developing, so it can't fly. It can still burn and break through any wall it wants to."

He took a step closer to Valentine. "It? What kind of it is *it*?" He had to know, even if he didn't really want to. Dread curdled in his stomach, and the memory of a very bad dream ripped through his mind.

"Dragon," Valentine answered.

Matter-of-fact. So fucking matter-of-fact. Too matter-of-fact for him to express any consternation, any disbelief. He wanted to deny the existence of dragons, but protesting about myths come to life was stupid when talking to a vampire.

"What do I need to know about dragons?" he asked, and guessed, "They breathe fire."

"And radiate high heat," she added. "They are the rarest of magical creatures. The most dangerous. The hardest to kill. They ought to be extinct, but dragon eggs are useful in certain kinds of magic." Her eyes blazed with anger as she added, "The sorcerers who risk using this kind of magic ought to be extinct. Well, the fool who used this egg is history. Apparently he used the egg in some sort of spell meant to control a vampire. Of course, using the dragon's egg made the spell so strong that it fucked over all the weaker vampires in the area. The magician really didn't know what he was doing. Unfortunately, he also didn't know that the egg needed to be properly disposed of after he used it. This dragon's freshly hatched, hungry, and on the move. It's going to bust out of the hotel, keep growing, getting hotter and hungrier all the while. It will take the city."

Why wasn't he surprised by this information? Valentine was also really old. Her explanation was probably colored by ancient thinking. "How big will it get?"

"Big."

"Can it fly?"

"Yes."

"Intelligent?"

"Cunning. Cruel. They also sort of imprint on the one who wakes them. Morgan Reese was not a nice man."

Nothing Valentine told him made Haven feel any

more confident. "What would be a good way to kill a dragon? Surface to air missiles? Call in an air strike from Nellis?"

She thought for a moment, then shook her head. "I wish. Dragons absorb energy. Being hit by explosives will only make it grow. It's a magical creature. Magic involves ritual. There is only one specific way to kill a dragon."

Haven wasn't going to like this. He really knew he wasn't going to like this. "Yeah?"

"We could use something to divert its attention. It would help if we had a virgin. Magical creatures are attracted to that sort of mortal. Unicorns want to be their pets. Dragons like the way they taste."

Haven wasn't sure if he should take her seriously. He said, "You want me to ask a bunch of cocktail waitresses for a volunteer?"

"Point taken." She quit stalling. "What we really need is a hero. A mortal hero." She looked around while she spoke, then her gaze came back to him. "Do you know how to use a sword?"

The speed with which she went from "we" to "you" was not lost on Haven.

"Yeah," he admitted grudgingly. "I can use a sword."

Valentine gazed at him with genuine pleasure and wonder. "You amaze me."

"I kill demons," he answered, facing the calculating hope in her look with gruff annoyance. "I've got all kinds of job skills."

"Do you have a sword?"

Haven ran through a mental inventory of the contents of the weapons locker back in the Jeep. He never went without firepower, explosives, and miscellaneous equipment, but he'd packed light this time.

"No," he told her. "In town for a wedding, not a beheading. How about a chainsaw? Would that work on a dragon?" The chainsaw was his weapon of choice when it came to demon killing. It had proved effective on vampires as well, though he wasn't about to mention that to Valentine.

Valentine chewed a nail and thought about it. "No," she decided. "Has to be a sword. Preferably a magical sword. Maybe they have something at the Excalibur that we—"

"Museum," Haven interrupted her. He jerked a thumb in the direction of the Silk Road's artifact display. "All the shit in there is real. I think I saw some weapons in the cases when she gave me the tour." He pulled the key card Murphy had given him out of his pocket. "Come on."

Chapter 20

HAVEN DIDN'T KNOW why he hurried forward, with Valentine close behind. He didn't want to get his hands on a magical sword. He was a monster slayer—but the monsters always tried to slay back. This was a dragon. A dragon.

He remembered his dream of fire. Premonition.

Monsters slayed back.

"Jesus," he muttered, his usually deep voice hoarse with fear.

A soft hand landed on his arm. Haven paused and turned to look into the concerned, ancient eyes of a little woman, whose lushly lovely face was framed by the singed ends of blue-black curls. "Every now and then the world needs a George," she said. "Tonight, it's you."

He got the reference. Hanging out with Char, he

couldn't help but learn stuff. "Was he real? Saint George?"

"He was very real."

"He really killed a dragon?"

"Yes."

"And?"

"Died in the process. They made him the patron saint of England, if that's any consolation."

Haven let out a low rumble of laughter. "Patron saint of Las Vegas?" That sounded appropriate, didn't it? "Let's go," he said, turning away from Valentine's touch. Thinking and talking about it weren't going to get the job done.

He led her to the side entrance to the museum. He swiped his card through the reader and the locks in the heavy door snapped open. There were bodies in the security room, sprawled on the floor and across work stations. One was still alive. Haven checked the monitor screens while Valentine took a moment to try to telepathically rouse the guard.

"No good," she said after the brief effort. "Anyone in the museum?"

"Looks clear."

"Feels that way, too. Odd. You'd think Ibis would send someone to guard the treasures. It's like he wants—" She cut herself off. "No time to worry about Ibis now." She gestured toward the inner door. "After you."

Haven used the key card again, and pushed the door open. Even though he hadn't detected any movement on the screens, and Valentine didn't detect anyone either. Haven had a bad feeling about the place. Maybe it was just all the magic trapped inside the cases that set off warning signals. He wondered if the power of Reese's spell had any effect on magical stuff so close to the epicenter. The wave of magic had certainly had an effect on other parts of town. It had woken up a dragon. What else had it woken up?

A roar sounded, far away, as they stepped into the subdued light and silky, silencing carpeting of the treasure room. Hearing the dragon in the distance didn't diminish the effect of being in here. There was a thrum and pulse of power in the place. It was like being inside an electrical generator. Haven made himself look into the display cases. The things in here were alive—or getting ready to be.

Haven stiffened into complete stillness, listening. Waiting.

The roar came again, just as distant, but this time a faint vibration shuddered through the building along with the noise. The temperature rose a few degrees, before the air-conditioning automatically compensated.

"It's on the move," Valentine said.

Haven gave her a sarcastic look. "You think?" The monster was going to escape out into the city. He looked around. "Where the hell did I see those swords?"

They split up, going down different aisles. He caught a glimpse of Valentine through the glass of one of the cases. It was like looking at her through water, or heat haze. What he saw was—amazing. So beautiful he had to look away.

Turning his head, he caught the gleam of tempered steel. He started toward the weapons case, but turned at the sound of metal and wood shattering. Alarms went off as the museum's main door opened. Haven braced himself, expecting the dragon. A woman walked in instead. Tall, slender, blond. He recognized her from tapes Murphy'd shown him. Not a woman, a vampire.

"Martina," he said.

"Really?" Valentine was suddenly beside him. She smiled, and it had fangs in it. "Cool."

Martina spotted them and stalked forward. "What are you doing here?"

Martina's attention was on Valentine. She ignored Haven, which was fine with him. He'd left his shotgun on the floor back by the door, but he'd make do with what he had if necessary. He fingered a trio of hollow stakes packed with explosives on his equipment belt.

Valentine stepped closer to the other vampire. "I'm looking for a way to save the fucking city. What are you doing here?" she questioned. She gestured around at all the cases, and Haven could feel all that potential energy focusing on her. "Looking for the scrolls, perhaps?" Val wondered. The amusement in her voice was scary. "Looking for other weapons to use against my children?"

This appeared to confuse Martina. "Save the city? Save mortals?"

"You have a problem with that?" Valentine asked.

"Mortals are your children?"

"In a way. Grandchildren, perhaps. Stepchildren. Maybe cousins. I care for them, too."

"Too?"

This woman really didn't get it. Haven left the vampires to face off each other and went to break into the sword case. He had to use one of the explosive stakes to do it, but the glass shattered quite satisfactorily, crumbling to the floor like an exploded windshield. There were a trio of swords to choose from inside the satin-lined case. Haven took the biggest, a greatsword, with a double-handed hilt and a jeweled pommel. Figures of twisting dragons were etched on the crossguard.

"Irony sucks," Haven muttered as he hefted the weapon. The sword was heavy, too, and not just with the weight of many pounds of sharpened steel.

When he turned back toward the vampires, they were still talking.

"I don't like the Enforcers much, either," Valentine said. "Or the Laws."

"Then—"

"You have no concept of reality, do you?" Valentine asked. "Don't know where you came from? Where the Enforcers came from?"

It bothered him that Valentine looked so relaxed, in a cat-playing-with-prey way. Martina was tense as hell, with claws jutting from the ends of her fingers. He didn't like the idea of a hostile vampire between him and the exits. There was a dragon out there.

"Time's wasting, Val," Haven called.

"You're right. Sorry," Valentine called back. "It won't take long, but I'm going to be formal about this."

"Formal?" Martina laughed. "What are you talking about, you silly girl?"

Valentine smiled, as if accepting a compliment from the other vampire. That Martina still hadn't recognized what Valentine was amazed Haven. Disgusted him as well. He hated that the bitch who'd started the trouble with the Enforcers was really, really stupid.

"I think she's a waste of your time," Haven told Valentine.

Valentine then took a deep breath as she straightened to her not particularly significant height. She held her hands up at shoulder height, palms facing out. Very much a ritual pose. For a second, Haven was reminded of the Snake Goddess amulet she wore.

Valentine spoke, slowly and clearly, her accent shifting to something that sounded kind of Greek to Haven. "Martina, blood daughter of Marco, of the line descended of Corvical."

"How did you know?" Martina demanded.

She snatched it out of your head, I bet, Haven thought.

Valentine continued speaking. "I declare you a danger to the Goddess's way. I declare you banished from the dark. I take your heart as mine."

Martina took a step back, still looking confused even as she completely vamped out into full fangs and claws. Valentine just stood there. Martina's muscles bunched. She sprang at the smaller woman.

What happened then was extremely fast, so fast

Haven had trouble following the action. It was also extremely bloody.

When the winner stepped back, Haven looked at the twitching body lying on the floor.

"You didn't take her heart."

"Wanted to give her a little time to think about her sins," Valentine answered as she wiped blood off her hands onto her short black skirt.

Haven looked around for Martina's missing head. When he found it, he saw that her eyes were open, her mouth moving. "She's not dead."

"She's dead. You get decapitated, you're dead. It'll take a few minutes for her consciousness to dissipate, though." When Valentine went on, Haven knew she was really speaking to the dying Martina. "I would like for her to understand that her trying to separate strigoi from Nighthawks was inviting chaos into a culture already on the edge of extinction. She wanted to live without limits, without laws."

"I thought you said the Laws are shit," Haven confronted Valentine.

"The Council's Laws don't concern me, but something older does," she answered. "I serve justice, Mr. Haven. Justice doesn't have anything to do with the law."

"You got that right," he agreed. He still didn't like the way the severed head continued to moan from where it had ended up wedged between two of the display cases. Magic hovered all around, like waiting ghosts, and the place reeked of fresh blood. The alarms still sounded.

Haven hefted the sword, squared his shoulders, and

said the last thing he wanted to say. "Dragon's waiting. Let's go."

"How do we get at it?" Haven questioned when he and Valentine reached the back of the crowd outside the hotel. People were gathered thickly on the street and sidewalk adjacent to a rear garden. They were clapping and pointing, laughing and gasping in wonder.

"How are they doing that?" was a common comment.

So was, "Cool special effect."

And, "Is that real fire?"

"Is this safe?" Haven heard someone say, though they didn't make any effort to leave.

"Did you see the way that tower fell down? I think that's real fire."

"They use real fire in the volcano at the Mirage," someone pointed out. "A dragon's cooler than a volcano."

"Not as cool as the pirate show."

Haven dragged his attention away from the onlookers. It was only a stalling technique, anyway. If people were stupid enough to stand around and gawk, it was their problem. Or possibly, it was Valentine's.

"Get everyone away from here," he ordered her, pleased at the role reversal for a moment.

Then he looked at the dragon.

"Holy shit."

He looked very closely, trying to decide if it was completely made out of fire. All he could tell was that it burned. He'd never thought much about dragons. He'd seen them on tattoos, and on artwork. Char read fantasy

novels. The covers of those books were full of dragons.
Mostly benign-looking creatures. The dragons in art
didn't blaze. This one had ruby red scales beneath the
fire. The scales themselves had a moving, molten qual-
ity to them. There were black patches dotted on the
scales, like lava crusting into obsidian. Its eyes were hot
gold, the expression in them the only thing cold about
the creature. The thing's form was all sharp angles of
claw and fanged snout, and sinuous, flowing body.
About twenty feet long, with a huge head. Haven could
sense it growing through the fur of flames and heat haze.
There were wings as well, flapping and uncurling, flapping and growing, emerging like the wings of a new-
born butterfly. "Will it fly?" he asked Valentine.

"Soon."

"Can it spout fire?"

"Soon," she answered again.

Haven decided it was futile to try to bull his way
through the crowd here at its thickest point. Even if he
tried waving the sword at the onlookers, they'd think it
was part of the show. So he turned around and moved
quickly back to the main hotel entrance. From there he
ran through the lobby and followed the smell of smoke
to the tower where the monster had been born, and had
then left in the most direct way possible. Haven had
glimpsed the gaping hole in the tower wall from the outside, and figured he could make his way through the
rubble if he followed the dragon's path. The dragon's attention had been on the crowd, and on scanning the busy
airport traffic that came in so close over the hotels.

Maybe it sensed the flying things as rivals, or prey. What Haven hoped was that he could sneak up on the monster's back while its attention was elsewhere.

Hurrying through the remains of the tower was hard. Broken walls formed barriers to climb and circumvent. The sprinkler system had kept the fire damage to a minimum, but it had also turned the floors into slippery streams, and created puddles in the wreckage that Haven had to wade through in almost complete darkness. He wished he had a sheath for the stupid, heavy sword, but he made do having to carry it.

The journey through the dark held its hazards, but it didn't go on for long. But even a few minutes alone in the dark gave him time to think. He thought about Char, and about how she was going to live forever, and he would never see her again. He thought about not getting out of this alive, and how there had been a time when he had gone into every fight for the thrill of it, never caring if he got out alive. He thought about the dream of dying by fire, and hoped to hell it wouldn't hurt as bad for real as it had in the dream. He thought about not having had the chance to say goodbye to her, but knew he didn't dare expend the energy to try for some sort of telepathic communication now. He thought about turning around and getting the hell out of Vegas. He even stopped for a moment, and muttered, "Fuck this." Then he shifted the sword in his sweating hands, and went on.

The dragon's trail led to the hole it had made in the side of the building, and the glow from the dragon itself illuminated the rest of the way to the garden.

Haven hesitated for only a moment when he reached the outside, to assess the ground before him and the whereabouts of the monster. It hadn't gone anywhere. Its wings were still unfolding. They were beautiful things, even still stunted and immature, made of fire and smoke. He wished now that he'd asked Valentine if she knew exactly how the mortal picked for the task slayed the dragon, but it was too late to check an instruction manual now. Watching the wings flutter and grow, he decided that maybe the spot between where they sprouted on the dragon's spine was a vulnerable point. Might as well make that the point of attack.

Besides, a large piece of the fallen tower wall jutted up from the ground near the dragon's back. Haven didn't have time to see whether the rubble would hold his weight. He didn't let himself think. He hefted the sword in his hands. He ran up the broken wall. He jumped on the dragon's back.

He exhaled as he landed feet first on the dragon's spine. The next breath he took burned his lungs. His clothes caught on fire as he landed on the creature's back. Haven screamed as skin melted and sloughed off his face and his hands. The world went up in pain.

For a hellish moment, Jebel Haven lost his mind, and was glad of it. If he was maddened by the agony, he could get on with dying and not have to struggle though any action that would make him linger in this burning world. Then dragon skin rippled beneath the melting soles of his boots. Wings fluttered, stirring burning ash through the air. Ash that was dying bits of Jebel Haven.

The knowledge woke him up, and pissed him off. If he was going to die, he had to die fighting. He didn't know any other way.

He didn't know how he kept his grip on the sword. In fact, the sword was the only thing in the world that was cool. While everything around him was flame, the weapon was cold steel ice. Haven felt the power of it, thrumming through him, stronger than the pain.

He had magic in him, right? An inborn ability to manipulate it? All he had to do was lift the sword. His arms couldn't do it, he already knew that.

Think.

He thought about lifting the sword. And the sword lifted his arms. The sword held him up. He thought about it some more, and the sword twisted, turned downward. The sword found the vulnerable spot. Jebel didn't see the exact place to strike, but the sword knew it. The sword urged him on, to gather all the strength he had in him.

The dragon turned its head to look at Haven, its golden eyes full of malevolent intelligence.

If he'd had any spit left in him, Jebel Haven would have spit in those eyes. As it was, he managed to croak, "Screw you."

And let the sword take the fall.

He plunged forward with it, tumbling into the spurting fountain of lava that was the wounded dragon's blood. He prayed for the world to go dark then, but instead it went very, very bright.

Chapter 21

IT WAS THE cool blue light, a small spot shining bravely amid the overwhelming fiery red, that drew Valentine's attention. She knew that the dragon didn't notice Haven, not at first. It knew instinctively that mortals were no danger to it. It had some of the arrogance of the magician that had brought it to life. The dragon wanted to grow its wings and fly. To breathe flame and burn the world. It was impatient, but it had no fear.

She knew fear, fear for a mortal man's life as she ignored the police cars and the fire trucks after making strong mental suggestions to direct their activity into an effort to save the hotel. She pretty much ignored the people that insisted on milling around. She'd gotten enough innocent bystanders to leave the area that she didn't feel guilty. Anyone who was stupid enough to hang around when a dragon was about deserved what they got. Flame rained down. Toxic fumes swirled along with the smoke and ash. Amid all that, a man faced living hell for the sake of them all.

Haven did not deserve what was happening to him. She could hear him screaming. She could smell his flesh. She could taste it in the ashes drifting on the wind. His blood bubbled and cooked.

And he fought. He would not give up. She knew that when the cold blue light appeared around him. She didn't think Haven knew what he was doing when he opened himself to the sacrifice and fed his soul into the sword. The sword, then, knew what to do. The cold light of the sword's power surrounded Haven, but it could shield him only a little. And a great deal of damage had already been done.

Valentine did not know when she began creeping closer. She wanted to help, wanted to do something. It wasn't fair that the rules of magic didn't work that way. Here she was, an ancient being of power and great wisdom—give or take a few really major fuckups—and all that the laws of magic allowed was for her to give advice and stand around and wa—

The flash of light blew away thought, blew away everything but awareness of light. Knocked her backward, and flat on her back.

The temperature dropped like a rock.

Thank the Goddess, was her first thought as she lay on the broken ground, staring up at the full moon over Las Vegas.

"Well, hasn't this been an interesting evening," she murmured.

It was all so big—the night, the world . . .

Then Valentine remembered Haven, and moved with the speed of lightning. She had to sprint across a layer of hot coals, the disintegrating remains of the dragon. Mortals wouldn't know it had existed, wouldn't know someone had saved their sorry asses. That was so unfair.

Haven still had the sword grasped in what was left of his hand. A faint crackle of blue energy ran over the metal and around Haven's burned and broken form. Valentine knelt in the warm ashes beside him. She ran her hand over him, sensing without touching.

She was a vampire; horror should not affect her. Making death was a craving. She was a Nighthawk, an eater of evil. She was thousands of years old, and had seen it all. This hurt. The death of a hero hurt.

Only he wasn't dead yet. The poor darling.

Near dead, yes. But she sensed the fading life in him. She sensed his awareness. He was pain. He was the longing for the ending of pain.

Valentine touched him, a finger almost hovering on his forehead. "Soon, sweetheart. Soon."

A word came back to her, communication filtered through the faint, gentle contact. *Why?*

The word took Valentine by surprise. And the sheer, stubborn cussedness that still made him cling to life despite the agony amazed her.

"Tenacious bastard," she said, sitting back on her heels. From this position, she studied what was left of him, rather than concentrating on the hideous wounds. He had a mouth left. His throat was intact.

It occurred to her that there was something she could do.

Once she made up her mind, Valentine didn't take time for gentleness. She grabbed Haven by the seared meat that had been his shoulders, and pulled his head into her lap. She extended mating fangs and bit deeply into her own wrist. Once blood was flowing freely, she pressed Haven's mouth against the wound. *Drink,* she thought at him. *Drink deep.*

Char. Even in this extremis, a picture of the other vampire formed in his mind. *Char—*

Drink deep and live. Valentine's command overrode any protest. Her blood was filling his mouth. Eventually, he swallowed. Once the taste of life was in him, he could not stop.

Valentine closed her eyes and whispered as she flowed into him, blending her life with another's. There had been enough evil magic in this place tonight. The words of power she drew out of long memory were life-giving, lifesaving, an act of love.

Desire roiled in her, hot as dragon fire. Desire awakened her. She could not taste him. She could not take him. She could only give, but how she wanted. Hunger bound her to him, as it would bind him to her. At another time, but very soon, she would take him into her the way he took her now. Then they would be lovers for as long a little while as the needs of their kind allowed.

* * *

"What has she done?"

Char felt the mating energy all around her as she ran across the field of ashes. It had been a garden not so long before. There had been darker energy here not so long ago. She recognized the residue of stubborn anger, and that was her Jebel. She was full of wonder at the way he'd expended magic in this place. And knew he had expended himself in the process. She had run here in tears, expecting to find her Jebel dead.

"What has she done?" Char questioned again, expecting no answer from Geoff, who ran at her side. She already knew what the bitch had done. What was happening right now.

Char crushed burnt flowers beneath her feet, as well as broken glass and charred bits of what had been one of the many towers of the Silk Road. Firefighters roamed through the ruins of the tower, onlookers gathered beyond a cordoned-off area across the street, but there were no mortals in the garden. Not exactly. Not anymore.

Jebel, Char grieved. *I should have been here to help him. It should be me.*

"He's mine!" she declared, coming upon where Valentine knelt with Jebel in her lap.

The old Nighthawk's head was thrown back, a look of longing and ecstasy transforming her beautiful face into something far more stunning. How could she compete with that?

"Damn you!" Char screamed, throwing herself forward.

Geoff caught Char around the waist, held on tight as she twisted and began to transform. The fury that surged from her hit him like a hammer blow, but he would not let her go.

No! he shouted into her mind, loud and commanding. He threw up a mental wall around Char and himself, holding her to her human shape with an effort that sent pain singing through him. *Do you want Haven dead? Do you want to die?*

He's mine!

Char McCairn was smart. She managed to fight down her instincts. "Let go of me," she said. They looked at each other for a few moments before she added, "Please." She was crying. It was the sign of a bereaved woman, not an angry vampire. Fury bubbled under the surface, but she had it together.

He didn't want to let her go. He wanted to hold her in his arms, maybe forever, but at least for a good, long now. But for the moment he stepped back, and kept his mouth shut. Haven's fate was a matter between Char and Valentine.

Valentine still cradled Haven in her lap, but he was no longer suckling. His eyes were closed, and her fingers stroked over the mottled red new skin of his cheeks, and forehead and lips.

Char stepped up to them and looked down at Jebel for a long time. He was unconscious, she could not touch his thoughts, but life was strong in him. He was injured still, weak as a kitten, but he was not the dying man she'd run across the city to find. He was healing. Another vampire's blood was doing that for him. Char hadn't thought the companion ritual could be used to save a life. But she knew that the ritual had taken Jebel from her life.

After a while she looked at Valentine. The old vampire gazed up at her with a dazed expression. There was no guilt in Valentine. No shame over what she'd stolen.

"He's mine," Char told her. "He's always been mine."

Valentine made the faintest gesture of negation. "He had no blood of yours in him. For which I thank you."

"Thank me?" Char heard her voice rise in bitter indignation. Her claws bit into her balled fists. She hated when Sterling's hands landed on her shoulders. He projected calm she didn't want, but she ended up relying on it anyway. "Thank me for waiting for him to make a choice?" she questioned again. "So it would be easier for you to steal him away?"

Valentine gave a faint shake of her head again. She seemed very tired. "Thank you, because if he had not been pure mortal, he could not have done what he had to do. He accepted the sacrifice," she went on. "Went willingly to certain death. He saved the city. That deserved a healing."

"Is that what you call it?" Char shouted at the woman. "You gave him your blood. He's mine!"

Behind her, Sterling whispered, "Not now."

Before her, Valentine said, "He is alive."

"Am I supposed to be comforted by that?" Was she supposed to be grateful? All Char felt was emptiness. Cheated. Betrayed. "You stole him." She'd never had a companion before. She hadn't wanted anyone but Jebel. They were partners, lovers, friends. "How could you—"

Valentine gently moved Jebel off her lap. She stood, very slowly. Her gaze was somewhere over Char's head. Char realized that the old Nighthawk's attention wasn't on her. It wasn't really on Jebel.

It was Sterling she spoke to when she said, "I'll be back in a few minutes."

"Val, you don't look so good. Do you need to go inside?" Sterling's solicitousness toward this companion thief galled Char.

"I am going inside," Valentine replied. She gestured, and Char couldn't help but look around, and up. The Silk Road was constructed of many towers and domes. Only one tower had been damaged by the dragon. Lights were on in other parts of the building. There was a circle of lighted windows at the very tip of the tallest tower. Valentine had forgotten Jebel. Her attention was now on the tower windows.

"Where are you going?" Sterling demanded as Valentine walked away.

"Someone wants to see me."

"Val—" Sterling began, sounding skeptical.

"Take him somewhere safe," Valentine cut him off. "I'll find you in a few minutes."

"Wait—!" Char called, but Valentine simply drew shadows around herself, and was gone.

Char loathed that she'd been dismissed. That she wasn't important. Valentine had taken the man she loved from her.

"Goddess damn it," she snarled. She shook off Sterling's hands and started toward Jebel. She snarled again when Sterling got to her injured lover first, and scooped Jebel up off the ground. "Leave him alone," Char demanded.

Sterling gave her a steady, stern look. "She told me to look after him."

"Do you always do what she tells you?"

Sterling didn't answer this. "Come on," he said. Cradling Jebel, he walked away.

Of course, she followed him. Geoff almost expected Char to attack him from behind. It took an effort to keep his muscles from tensing. He made himself calm, relaxed, neutral. He was not going to gloat over his good fortune, not while the hurt was so fresh for Char. She was still crying, bitter salt perfumed her skin. The tang of it burned in his nostrils and throat. Meanwhile, Haven slept in his arms, feverish, his body gaunt beneath Geoff's hands. The man had been through literal hell, and was lucky to be alive. Geoff hoped he could make Char see it that way.

They covered themselves in shadows until they reached the front entrance of the hotel. Yellow tape roped off the lobby doors, but there was no one around. The whole building had been emptied of mortals, though the excitement had all been elsewhere. Geoff sensed the hidden presence of vampires inside. They were all neatly hidden away in secret places the firefighters would never find. They could stay hidden for-

ever, for all he cared, as long as no one tried to interfere
with his and Char's presence here.

Geoff carried Haven into the lobby and settled him on
a couch covered in red and gold silk, beneath a canopy
of equally brightly colored cloth. There was a low
gilded table and three deep chairs grouped with the
couch.

Geoff settled into one of the chairs, realized he was
weary, and wondered at the time. The approach of dawn
was something his kind naturally sensed, but the events
of this night had driven his time sense completely
askew. He tensed as he checked his watch, and sighed in
relief. It was not as late as he'd feared. He sat back
against the thickly cushioned chair back.

"Hell of a night," he said. Excitement still buzzed in
him, and the thrill of the hunt.

"Hell of a night," Char answered.

The sadness in her voice brought Geoff out of the
brief sense of pleasure at jobs well done.

He sat up, and found that she'd taken a seat on the
couch. Haven's head was in her lap, her fingers stroking
the salt and pepper stubble of hair left on his head. Geoff's first impulse was to point out that Valentine would
not like this intimacy. But he managed to keep his
mouth shut on the matter, even though Char gave him a
look that dared him to make the comment.

He did say, "You have to accept the situation."

"Why?" she shot back, spoiling for a fight.

"All right." He tried again. "You don't have to like it,

but you have to live with it. Haven belongs to Valentine. She didn't do it to hurt you. She did it to save his life."

Char quivered with rage, but she gave a sharp nod. "I know that. It should have been me. She should have waited."

"I doubt there was time to wait. She could have let him die," he added. "But you wouldn't want her to have done that."

"I—" She shook her head. "I don't know. I don't want him with anyone but me. But I don't want him to die."

"Then Valentine did the only thing that would save him. He'll be one of us now, Char. But he won't be your bloodchild," he went on, as persuasive as he could be. "Think about that. If you don't make him into a vampire, you won't have to worry about incest. The pair of you can be together. Forever. As Nighthawks." *And you can be with me until then,* he thought. *It could be decades, even centuries. Depends on how long before Haven feels the need to change to Nighthawk.*

She glared at him, still shocked by his believing that Nighthawks were different, were beyond the rules of regular vampire life. She didn't want to believe, but now she had a reason to start thinking about the situation. It was an excuse to hold out hope that she and her beloved Jebel could still be together.

She continued to stare at him, her hands on the other man. "Think about new possibilities," Geoff urged.

"Leave us alone," was Char's response.

Geoff shook his head. Now was not the time to push her. "Fine."

He got up and walked away. Might as well give her time to get used to the idea. Time to say goodbye.

Curiosity led him toward the scent of magic mixed with smoke. He glanced into the theater, and tasted the air. Dark magic permeated the place, centered on the empty stage. A human had died there, and a vampire had done the killing. Geoff wondered what that was about. The resident vampires must have taken care of the mess, because there was no physical sign of violent death in the auditorium.

Geoff backed out of the room, and continued following scent. It led him into the damaged tower, where he splashed through occasional puddles and dodged emergency lighting. There were still firefighters around, and rescue workers making a cautious, slow search of the premises. Geoff cautiously made sure that none of them saw him. He eventually found his way to a room where the dregs of magic hit his senses like the stench of a rotting corpse.

Again, any traces of death, or supernatural dealings, had been wiped away, but Geoff could tell that this was where horrible things had occurred. He wondered if the hotel vampires had spread their cleanup assignment to the mess running amok on Fremont Street. The mortals working that emergency could certainly use help in hiding evidence.

Instead of backing away from the ugly vibes that still lingered in the place, Geoff was drawn to explore. It was a large room. Geoff guessed that it had served as a dressing room and storage area for the late stage magi-

cian. He moved aimlessly from object to object for a
while. Everything was wet. Everything smelled burned.
The place reeked of evil. It occurred to him that if the
dragon had been born here, the place should be more
damaged. It also occurred to him that there was a reason
the place was mostly untouched. Something magical
was still in the room. It had protected itself from the fire.
And it was calling to him.

Geoff stopped in the middle of the room, and considered options. Magic was something to use. You couldn't
let magic use you. Valentine would say that that was just
spoiling it. Still, one shouldn't look gift horses in the
mouth, either.

So, Geoff let the magic call him across the room to
where fire-damaged furniture leaned at odd angles
around a fire-blackened coffee table. Resting on one of
the damaged chairs was a blue plastic notebook. It was
cool to the touch when he picked it up. There was no
sign of any damage to the notebook, or the paper inside
it. It was far heavier in his hand than it should be. And
there was a subvocal hum emanating from it. The hum
held an invitation to look inside, and discover the secrets of the universe.

Geoff didn't take the spell book up on its invitation.
"Not yet," he said. This was not the time or the place to
study a spell book. Everyone, and *everything*, that had
been part of tonight's disasters needed a cooling-off pe-
riod. Once he was calm, ready, and well away from this
epicenter of magic, Geoff thought he might peruse the
object that had given itself to him.

He tucked the notebook under his arm, and walked back to the lobby. Once back at the spot where he'd left Char and Haven, he stopped for a moment to take a frustrated look at the couch. He shook his head thoughtfully, but said and did nothing.

He sat down in the deep, comfortable chair, and waited for Valentine to return.

Chapter 22

"GOOD EVENING, MADAM."

Valentine looked at the obsequious minion waiting for her by the elevator, and sneered. *Good evening, madam? What was that about?*

"If madam will come with me, please."

She stepped out of the carpeted private elevator car and into a hallway. The walls were of shining black marble, the floor was bright white. When she felt the coolness of the polished stone against the soles of her feet, she looked down and noticed that she wasn't wearing shoes. It took Valentine a moment to remember that she'd found it easier to run across the hot ashes to Jebel barefoot than in slippery, grit-filled sandals. Chalk up a pair of shoes Ibis owed her, along with all the other aggravations of this night.

"Madam?" He was dressed, and sounded, like a butler. Except that he was dressed all in black. He even had a very upper-crust British accent.

She wasn't in the mood for niceties. She waved a hand at the butler. "Shoo."

He bowed, and backed up a few steps, almost disappearing against the shining black marble of the walls, except for a pale face that stood out like a thumb. "As madam wishes."

This left Valentine to her own devices in finding Ibis, but that was hardly difficult. Ibis had requested her presence; she had but to follow his mental trail down the hall, through a large meeting room, and through a door into a private office. She spotted other black-clad retainers outlined against the wall and the tall windows along the way. They all exuded an air of obsequious helpfulness that set her fangs on edge. But all this alert, respectful *niceness* was a hallmark of Ibis's style.

"You're laying it on thick," Valentine said when she opened the door and stepped into the inner sanctum of one of the few vampires older, and shorter, than herself. He also wore more makeup, but he'd never lost his Prince of Egypt manner.

"I was never a prince," he corrected her thought. "Merely a humble vizier, high priest, physician, and royal architect. These days I dabble in being an archivist and businessman."

"And troublemaker."

He inclined his head slightly. "Declare me one, if you must."

"Your credentials remain impressive."

"Thank you, Lady of Snakes."

Valentine frowned at the title, but she crossed her hands over her breasts and inclined her head piously. "I am but a retired servant of that Lady."

"And of the Other Lady? Our Lady?"

"I've been known to come out of retirement to do her bidding."

"As you did tonight."

He was sitting with his back to the high, wide windows. The view was disconcerting, but Valentine wasn't going to let it get to her at this point. She plopped into a comfortable leather chair opposite Ibis, and stared across the wide glass-topped desk at him. The desk reflected the city lights. The room was dark, but for the glow of the neon, the moon, the stabbing beacon rising from the tip of the Luxor pyramid, and their reflections.

"What do you think of the Luxor?" she asked. "Remind you of home?"

"I quite like the place," he answered. "They have the colors right. That's a hotel design I would have gone with if it hadn't already been done. Recreating the city has proved more useful." His smile was sly, his whole attitude very, very smug. "And fun."

Fun. Ibis called all the chaos fun? "What is up with you?" she demanded.

The little, shaven-headed vampire folded his sturdy, workman's hands together on the desk top. "Blood-wine?" he asked politely.

She grimaced. "I don't drink that shit." She looked at

the servant hovering attentively by the door. "Get me some coffee."

The minion bowed and immediately hustled off to do her bidding. She smiled after the servant. "Do you ever get up and do anything for yourself?" she asked Ibis.

When she looked back at him, he shrugged. "I like keeping a few layers of functionaries between myself and any project I initiate. Be it pouring a cup of coffee—"

"Or causing a hell of a lot of damage to strigoi society," she finished for him.

He shrugged again. "Damage? I have caused no damage. I have harmed none." He smiled, crinkling up the corners of his artfully painted eyes. "Who have *I* harmed personally with this night's activities?"

It was Valentine's turn to shrug. "How about your investors?" She waggled a finger at him. "I own some stock in this property. If I lose money because of the fire—"

Ibis put up a hand to silence her. "You will lose nothing. I will pay for the necessary repairs out of my own pocket. In fact, the media will praise the safety precautions taken by the hotel in isolating any possible fire damage. No one was hurt, no guest's property was damaged. The Silk Road's reputation will be enhanced rather than trashed."

"You planned to damage the hotel?"

"Don't I always plan for everything? Let's say, damage to the property was factored in to the actions I foresaw taking place."

Ibis was a seer of great ability, Valentine finally recalled. "You had a vision of tonight's proceedings?"

"I did. And then I set the events to fulfill that vision in
motion," he admitted. "It seemed like a good idea. My
public relations team is already spinning the story to put
the blame for the fire on the late Mr. Morgan Reese. He
will be found to have been most unstable and reckless.
Which he was, of course." Ibis smiled. "That was why I
had him hired. He was quite a perfect pawn."

The servant brought back her coffee, and a glass of
wine for Ibis, then faded into the shadows again. Valentine sat back and savored the scent of the coffee, and the
texture of the bone china cup. She was tired, drained,
but there was a thrum of excitement beneath the layers
of stress and strain.

"The call to adventure," Ibis said. "It has always been
part of you."

"I'm retired," she reminded him. "I write scripts. I've
started a novel. I don't try to change the world."

"You did try not so long ago," he said. "Remember
the original script for *If Truth Be Told*?"

She didn't ask how he knew about her having tried to
out the Enforcer of Los Angeles. She'd convinced herself that trying to tell a little bit of truth about the current
state of the vampire world had been an aberration, not a
small act of rebellion. "I had writer's block. It was only
a plot for a low-budget horror movie. Nobody would
have believed it." She drained the very hot coffee in a
long gulp, then put the cup down carefully on the glass

desk top. "Writing about Selim's life wasn't the same as your building a hotel based on the lost city."

"Yes, it was."

"I didn't get to make the movie, though, did I?"

"The Enforcer of Las Vegas was more lax in his duties than the Hunter of Los Angeles. You should have written about Duke instead. You still could. A movie about a corrupt cop coming to a bad end might be interesting."

"Been done recently. With Denzel. You haven't seen *Training Day*, have you?"

"Did it have corrupt vampire cops? Did it have a young Nighthawk couple struggling against outmoded taboos as the love interests?"

She shook her head.

"There's a convention center full of producers in Las Vegas this week, Valentia," Ibis went on. "I knew you'd be in town for it. Why don't you pitch this corrupt vampire cop picture to them?"

Ibis had always been seductive. She hadn't fallen for it for a few thousand years. "What is your agenda this time?" she demanded. "What is your problem?"

"My agenda is the same as always. Truth for all. Knowledge is power. Equality for the masses."

"Oh, Goddess," she muttered. "Here we go again."

"You used to agree with me."

"I agreed that the city was a decadent cesspit, but did I help you destroy it?"

"The Mongols destroyed it from without," he said. "And rebellion by the abused companions from within."

"And we both know who the brains behind both attacks was."

He put a finger to his lips. "My dear—"

"Did it do any good?" she demanded. "We both know that it did not. The survivors went even more conservative. They abandoned the old ways completely. Did they return to being protectors of the mortals and treating companions as cherished lovers? No, they did not. Out of fear they enslaved companions with even stricter rules that bound them as property. They organized the Nighthawks—my children—as servants to their new Council, to their petty, perverse, inflexible Laws of the Blood."

"And while *they* messed up *our* society, *you* did what?" he questioned.

Valentine let out her breath in a deep whoosh. She knew better than to get up on a high horse with Ibis. "Hey, I tamed Istvan," she replied, pointing out at least one proactive action in the last few hundred years. "He would have killed every vampire on the planet if I hadn't had a talk with him."

"He ended up working for the Council."

"Which did need someone who could take out any Enforcers that went bad. Even the Strigoi Council has a few good ideas. They have kept the underneath together."

"They've kept a stranglehold on our society. There's nothing but repression. There's been no growth, no change, no adapting to modern times. They teach our kind to enslave, but not to love. I will agree that most of

the Enforcers have fought for justice. They have punished evil. They remain your children, though most of
them don't even know you exist, dear Lady Valentia.
The Council hasn't corrupted them. It's time you came
out to lead the Nighthawks again."

"Oh, no, it isn't."

"Once the strigoi population knows about the Scrolls
of Silk, and Martina's scientific data, the Nighthawks
will have to justify their existence. They'll need you to
organize them."

Valentine was on her feet. She leaned forward, her
hands flat on the desk. Glaring at Ibis. "You let that information out? Martina was working for you?"

"She did not knowingly cooperate with my plans," he
answered. "Martina didn't *know* much about anything.
But her self-centered stupidity made her useful."

Valentine scraped her claws loudly across the polished glass. She got some satisfaction at Ibis's wincing
at the sound. "You know, I think maybe I ripped off the
wrong head this evening."

"Don't be peevish, Valentia."

"My name is Valentine. I don't do revolutions."

He was totally unfazed by any declaration she might
make. "Then perhaps your Geoffrey will take the proper
actions. Perhaps Char will. Perhaps Haven will. Each
has their own goals. They are freedom fighters. Each
came to the Silk Road looking for something. Haven
wants to help the companions," he informed Valentine.
"Char wants to be a superhero, to protect the world of

day as well as the world of night. Geoffrey is a modern man. He cannot and will not be trapped in the past. I built the Silk Road for them. All they had to do was come to me and ask for whatever they needed. Of course, they suspected a trap."

"They're smart kids."

"And I built the Silk Road mostly for you."

"Bullshit."

"I used Martina. I used Reese. I used poor Ben Siegel and his companion, which I do regret. I did what I had to do to start the revolution—"

"Without getting caught," she interrupted his practiced little speech.

He sat back, and folded his hands again. "Of course. I never get caught."

She held up an index finger. "Excuse me, but I would say that you are well and truly busted."

"Not by you," he said, utterly confident. "If you kill me, it will be a victory for the Council. You'd never let them win a big one. You know the world needs me. Someday, some way, I will change vampire society back to the way the Goddess meant for us to be. We are meant to work our way back to the light by doing good. Young Char has the right ideas. So do Haven and his online crew."

"His what?"

Ibis was on a roll, and wasn't going to be deflected from his preaching by any questions from her. "So does Geoff." He leveled his dark, intense, persuasive gaze at her. "So do you. I can shape the pattern. It is up to others to bring the pattern to life."

"You're as agoraphobic as I am," she realized.

"Worse." He blinked, having deviated from his script. "I can look outside, but can't bear to go out. Everywhere I go, I go in spirit form." He took a moment to look at the lights reflected in the desktop, then raised his gaze to her once more. "Where was I?"

"Revolution. Blah, blah, blah."

"What do you think it means?" he asked softly. "The Law that says 'Beware of the Light'?"

She gestured toward the bright, bright, beautiful city of light behind them. "I've seen what that does to the neon junkies."

He shook his head. "I don't think that's the light the Law means. I think the light *they* want us to beware of is the light of knowledge."

"Bullshit," she replied.

"When did you get to be so reclusive?" he questioned. "So—uninvolved?"

Valentine thought about it, and frowned. "You know, I don't quite remember. When the psychics started dying, maybe. That—hurt."

"It was the fourteenth century," he said, nodding gravely. "You had to be there."

"It's not the fourteenth century anymore," she added, because she knew he would.

"I could use your help again tonight."

His expression and tone had changed. He wasn't talking about anything to do with his revolution now. Valentine relaxed, remembered that she was tired, and sat back in the comfortable leather chair. "What?"

"You did the right thing when you let Ben kill Reese."

"Are you implying that I don't generally do the right thing?"

"You're a lazy flake," he said. "That's the truth, not an implication."

"Now you're insulting me? Me, who holds your life in my hands."

"You do, of course. But you won't take it."

"Why not?"

"You know how fattening I'd be. You've always watched your figure. And now that you work in Hollywood . . ."

"You insult me," she said, forcibly keeping to a more formal tone. "You, who have never been anything but a troublemaker. And who is not even a Nighthawk."

"Not even?" His heavily arched eyebrows went up. There was amusement in his dark eyes. She never had been able to scare him. No one could. "Do I detect a hint of racial prejudice in your tone, my pretty Valentia?"

"Snobbery," she countered.

She wished he'd stop calling her by that name. It wasn't even her real name, but a version of it that she'd adopted sometime in the Roman era because her then companion had found her ancient name too hard to pronounce. Having had his tongue cut out before he was forced to be a gladiator hadn't helped his speech. Ibis, at least, knew her real name. As she knew his.

"I'm too old to be a Nighthawk," Ibis reminded her. "You should respect your elders, youngster."

"Is this how you ask for a favor?" They'd always enjoyed bickering with each other, though right now she wasn't sure why she found it pleasant to spar with Ibis. She pulled back from their old pattern, and asked, "What do you want?"

He chuckled. No doubt at her *this had better be good* tone. "It's Ben," he told her. "The vampire who killed Reese. Reese was a creature invested with great power. Ben has eaten that power, and it is starting to change him."

Change him how? she started to ask, then realized. "He's a child of mine."

"He needs your help to be reborn."

She gave Ibis a hard look. "You planned this, too, didn't you? To distract me from punishing you?"

"It's a distraction," he agreed. "It will give you time to calm down. Not that I really believe you would punish me for doing the right thing."

"I hate when you're like this."

"I know." His features creased in a devilish grin. "But wasn't the fall of the Roman Empire fun?"

"Yeah—but those were mortals we punished, not our own kind."

"Then shame on us for not—"

"Enough!" Valentine held up her hand for silence. She sighed. "Where is this Ben person?"

"My people have him safe. Shall I take you to him?" He started to come around the wide desk.

Valentine shook her head. "Not tonight. I'm sorry if he's suffering, but I'm not up to any more blood rituals tonight."

"Ah, yes." Ibis nodded gravely. "Mr. Haven. That was a good thing you did."

"Yeah. His girlfriend doesn't think so."

She looked out the windows. The world was wide and open, and scary, but from up here it didn't seem so big. The lights were so pretty. She was so tired, and everything was complicated. She needed a day to sleep, really sleep, to dream rather than to think. Sometimes the answers came in dreams. "I want a bedroom," she said to the man who owned the hotel. "The best room in the house."

He bowed his bald head gravely. "Of course. You deserve only the best."

"Tomorrow I'll take care of your Ben."

"I have your promise?"

"Yes. Of course." As if she would ever deny a rebirth to one of her children. "Las Vegas is going to need a new Enforcer, I suppose."

"A new Guardian of the Night." Ibis used one of the Nighthawks' old titles. "Defender. Protector. A Hunter for the territory. Tytan. Bu—"

"Oh, shut the fuck up."

He bowed. "As the Lady of Snakes wishes."

"That isn't shutting up." Valentine turned around. She glanced at the nearest silently watching vampire servant. "I'm going to the lobby first. Then you can show me to my suite." She glanced back at Ibis. "I'll decide what to do about you tomorrow."

Ibis put a finger over his closed mouth, deliberately provoking her by obeying her. In response, she tossed what was left of her long, curling hair, and walked out.

Geoff stood as Valentine approached, trailed at a distance by another vampire. From the look on her face and the vibes she put out, Geoff thought it might be wise to be circumspect. Instead, he put himself between her and the view of the couch.

"What's up?" he asked. "Where have you been? What's going on?"

"Where's Jebel?" she asked, peering past him at the empty sofa. "Where's the girl?"

Anger flared white hot in her, but Geoff stayed directly in front of her. "Gone," he said.

"I see that. Where?"

"I have no idea." Geoff reached out to touch her shoulder. She felt very tired. "Can't you feel him?"

Her gaze snapped to his, accusing. "When?"

"I have no idea." He spoke the absolute truth. "I was looking around the building. When I came back, they were gone."

"You let her go."

"I'm not Char's keeper." He sure as hell wasn't Haven's.

Fury bubbled through her, and jealousy. It seethed beneath the exhaustion. "I'm going to kill her."

"No, you're not." It was another statement of fact, and a declaration of intent. He kept his hand on Valentine's shoulder, knowing she wanted to pull away, to run out into the night and find the mortal that now belonged to her. Geoff projected calm, reason, and sympathy for this sudden loss.

"Why doesn't anyone believe me when I say I'm going to kill them?" Valentine asked. She sounded petulant, but there were tears in her eyes. "He's mine," she added.

"Char can't see it that way. Not yet. She's hardly going to hurt Haven, Val." She glared at him. Silent, seething. "Let me go after her," Geoff suggested. "Let me handle it."

His words were a reminder that he had handled a great deal for her in the last several years. She depended on him. He'd helped her take steps out into the world again, but had been a shield and anchor as well. He also remembered that she and Haven had yet to complete the companion bond. Haven was not completely Valentine's yet.

"I will definitely make sure he comes back to you," Geoff promised his friend and mentor.

She recognized his sincerity, and she smiled a little. "For all my reasons, and for yours."

He tilted his head in acknowledgment. "As long as I bring him back . . ."

She didn't like it, but he felt the shoulders beneath his hands slump in acquiescence. She gave a brief look at the vampire that had followed her across the lobby, and now stood waiting patiently away from them. Then she looked back at Geoff. "Ibis knew," she told him. "Ibis always knows what's going on. Ibis arranges what's going on."

"Ibis?"

"Never mind. He's my problem. So's turning a vampire into a Nighthawk. Ibis made me promise to do that little job tomorrow night."

Geoff tried not to show any relief. "Then you can't go after Char. Not if you have to—"

"Don't keep piling it on, sweetie. We both know you get the job."

Geoff drew Valentine into a quick, hard hug. "It's going to be okay," he promised her. "Everything's going to be okay."

She stepped away from him. "I seriously doubt that. Just—Beware of the Light, okay?"

Maybe she'd noticed that he was no longer wearing sunglasses. "I will," he promised.

"Fine." She turned toward the waiting vampire. "I'm going to bed now."

Geoff stood in the otherwise empty lobby and watched her follow her guide toward the elevators. He wanted to make sure she was out of sight before he pulled the spell book out from under the chair cushion where he'd stashed it. He found it very interesting that the book had remained dormant while he talked to Valentine.

He was certain he could pick up Char's psychic scent. Certain he could catch up to her. He wasn't yet certain what to do or say to get her to let Jebel Haven go. He'd come up with something when the time came.

Valentine's guide directed her toward a corridor. The last thing that Valentine did before she disappeared from sight was send a thought Geoff's way.

Don't make me have to track you down, the words filled his head. *Because I really don't want to have to kill you.*

Is that any way to say goodbye to a friend? Geoff thought back.

It is if you're a vampire, was her answer.